Cover Design: Len Gibbs
Front Cover Illustration: Willow Creek
Back Cover Illustration: Shelling Peas

2nd printing, November, 1988
© Copyright Len Gibbs, 1988

Canadian Cataloguing in Publication Data

Gibbs, Len 1929
    Images: thirty stories by favorite writers

2nd printing

ISBN 1-55021-007-6

1. Short stories, Canadian (English) - 20th century.* I. Gibbs, Betty.

PS8321.I53 1988   C813'.01'08   C88-094549-4

PR9197.32.I53 1988

We would like to thank the Ontario Arts Council and the Canada Council for their assistance in the production of this book.

New Canada Publications, a division of NC Press Limited, Box 4010, Station A, Toronto, Ontario, Canada, M5W 1H8.

Printed and bound in Canada

Thirty Stories by Favorite Writers

IMAGES

Paintings by LEN GIBBS

NC PRESS LIMITED 1988

THE STORIES

THE PLATES

INTRODUCTION

In this book there are reproductions of paintings and excerpts from thirty stories by well known authors. The two are not made for each other. They were created in different places at different times, and yet they have a common bond for they all celebrate the lifestyle of people who have chosen to live in remote and forgotten places.

Without the conveniences of urban living they are a self-sufficient group accepting with a sense of joy, the discipline and skills that must be learned to survive or wrest a living from an unyielding land. They tell their tales with love and humor and with respect and sorrow.

The short selections included in this book were not written to enhance Len Gibbs paintings, nor were the paintings executed to illustrate the prose. It is a happy concidence that the two art forms meld so well together.

Bright, Shining Days

Rhythms of the Land
Robert Collins

The wind and sky orchestrated our moods. The wind played the tunes, the sky lit the stage. Together they could make us laugh or cry. When the sun shone, our spirits turned to green and gold. I lay in the yard on my back, staring deep into the sky until it whirled and spun me with it.

The clouds came, legion upon legion, darkening the pasture sloughs and casting shadows on our souls. We looked to the sky for portents. Did that black cloud carry rain or dust or hail? Would that change of moon from Full to Last Quarter, as noted on the Wheat Pool calendar, bring a change of weather? My father often thought it would, and the moon proved him right often enough.

And the wind? It never rested. It strummed the telephone wires; I pressed my face hard against the poles, rubbed silvery gray by the years, and listened to their song. The wind ebbed and flowed through the whispering poplars, churned up blizzards, flung clouds pell-mell to Manitoba. Its rough hand riffled the heads of wheat and foxtail. It lashed the stagnant water in Long Slough, booted prickly balls of Russian thistle end over end, and lifted the tail feathers of matronly hens who clucked with embarrassment. Some people were driven to suicide by the wind. Some of us were soothed by it, and still are.

I knew so intimately the smells and tastes, the language and rhythms of the land, that even now, if I were dropped there not knowing time or date, I could say, "This is a February afternoon because the long shadows always slant off the sharp snowdrifts, just so, at four o'clock," or "This is August because August always smells of sage grass and ripening wheat."

The seasons ran their cycles, as sure as life and death. Spring was best, with its sudden, softer kiss of wind, its first crows hacking and coughing in the treetops. Then a rush of warblers, flickers, swallows, blackbirds, ducks and grebes, once a robin, a bluebird, even a Baltimore oriole, all with their madrigals of hope.

The meadowlarks hunched on fence posts, drab and round shouldered until they sprang into the sky with a flash of brown ascot and golden breast. Redwing blackbirds bickered in creaky-hinge voices. Great broad-winged hawks came from sledding down the wind, their shadows panicking our squawking hens. Gophers rose up from winter hibernation with their cheerful dumb-guy expressions, and welcomed the sunshine into their hides.

The earth was fragrant with new, green life. I dug my grubby fingers into soil built up, grain by grain, from ancient seabeds and by restless glaciers a zillion sunsets ago. It came up in my fist, a damp, crumbly ball, our hope for another year.

If we were lucky, rain came after the seed was in, turning the gumbo roads to pudding and filling sloughs to their brims, until the farmers' tobacco-stained smiles cracked through their three-day whiskers. Yes! Maybe *this* would be the year, by God, the year of the bumper crop!

HARD TIMES

(overleaf) This man is a favorite model. He's an actor with a wonderfully expressive face. Here he captured exactly what I wanted to paint . . . the desperate yearning in the hands and the hopelessness in his wind-worn eyes. We searched a long time for his authentic 1930's collarless shirt, worn overalls and battered fedora.

On the Fly
Jayne Heese

F rom somewhere in the distance came the throb of an engine. A combine was plying the swaths of a ripe harvest. On the air, the smell of wheat was heady. Mounds of the golden stuff filled the box behind me.

The drone of the combine grew louder as first the auger, then the cab, then the whirling pickup crested the horizon. A light blinked. My signal.

I turned the key. The truck's engine turned over and roared to life. The lumbering vehicle rolled forward as I eased the clutch off.

It was exciting. It was my first time. I was going to "take it on the fly," as my dad had put it. Combine and truck would move along together, the grain would pour into the box without a halt in the progress of the harvest.

I drove forward in anticipation. The combine came toward me. I could see Dad's face through the dusty glass of the cab. Was he wondering if I could do it?

We met and passed. When I could see the twirling spreader in my rear view mirror, I wheeled the truck around, picked up speed and crept up behind the labouring thresher. I drew up beside the machine finally, its pulleys and churning belts visible through the passenger window. I checked over my shoulder. The auger's spout was poised over the front half of the box. I struggled to keep the speed of my truck even with that of Dad's combine. I felt a thrill of accomplishment when I heard the sudden whir of the auger turning and the swish of grain as it tumbled into the box. Elated, I did a little jumping wiggle in my seat, mindful not to stray off my course however.

Checking over my shoulder once more, I could see the pile rising higher. I eased off the accelerator ever so slightly to position the auger over the rear, less full portion of the grain box. Only a few short moments later the auger clattered as the combine hopper ran empty and the last of the kernels trickled out of the spout.

With a grin as wide as the breadth between my ears would permit, I gunned the engine and headed for the yard where I would empty the load.

Later that evening, when the swathes were taking on the night dew and the combine would have to be put to rest until morning, Dad would climb down from his perch, clap me on the shoulder and say, "Good girl." And that would be enough for me.

April Passage
Farley Mowat

It was raining when I woke, a warm and gentle rain that did not beat harshly on the window glass, but melted into the unresisting air so that the smell of the morning was as heavy and sweet as the breath of ruminating cows.

By the time I came down to breakfast the rain was done and the brown clouds were passing, leaving behind them a blue mesh of sky with the last cloud tendrils swaying dimly over it. I went to the back door and stood there for a moment, listening to the roundelay of horned larks on the distant fields.

It had been a dour and ugly winter, prolonging its intemperance almost until this hour, and giving way to spring with a sullen reluctance. The days had been cold and leaden and the wet winds of March had smacked of the charnel house. Now they were past. I stood on the doorstep and felt the remembered sun, heard the gibbering of the freshet, watched little deltas of yellow mud form along the gutters, and smelled the sensual essence rising from the warming soil.

Mutt came to the door behind me. I turned and looked at him and time jumped suddenly and I saw that he was old. I put my hand on his grizzled muzzle and shook it gently.

"Spring's here, old-timer," I told him. "And who knows—perhaps the ducks have come back to the pond."

He wagged his tail once and then moved stiffly by me, his nostrils wrinkling as he tested the fleeting breeze.

The winter past had been the longest he had known. Through the short-clipped days of it he had lain dreaming by the fire. Little half-heard whimpers had stirred his drawn lips as he journeyed into time in the sole direction that remained open to him. He had dreamed the bitter days away, content to sleep.

As I sat down to breakfast I glanced out the kitchen window and I could see him moving slowly down the road toward the pond. I knew that he had gone to see about those ducks, and when the meal was done I put on my rubber boots, picked up my field glasses, and followed after.

The country road was silver with runnels of thaw water, and bronzed by the sliding ridges of the melting ruts. There was no other wanderer on that road, yet I was not alone, for his tracks went with me, each pawprint as familiar as the print of my own hand. I followed them, and I knew each thing that he had done, each move that he had made, each thought that had been his; for so it is with two who live one life together.

The tracks meandered crabwise to and fro across the road. I saw where he had come to the old *Trespassers Forbidden* sign, which had leaned against the flank of a supporting snowdrift all the winter through, but now was heeled over to a crazy angle, one jagged end tipped accusingly to the sky, where flocks of juncos bounded cleanly over and ignored its weary threat. The tracks stopped here, and I knew that he had stood for a long time, his old nose working as he untangled the identities of the many foxes, the farm dogs, and the hounds which had come this way during the winter months.

We went on then, the tracks and I, over the old corduroy and across the log bridge, to pause for a moment where a torpid garter snake had undulated slowly through the softening mud.

There Mutt had left the road and turned into the fallow fields, pausing here and there to sniff at an old cow flap, or at the collapsing burrows left by the field mice underneath the vanished snow.

So we came at last to the beech woods and passed under the red tracery of budding branches where a squirrel jabbered its defiance at the unheeding back of a horned owl, brooding somberly over her white eggs.

The pond lay near at hand. I stopped and sat down on an upturned stump and let the sun beat down on me while I swept the surface of the water with my glasses. I could see no ducks, yet I knew they were there. Back in the yellow cattails old greenhead and his mate were waiting patiently for me to go so they could resume their ponderous courtship. I smiled, knowing that they would not long be left in peace, even in their secluded place.

I wait and the first bee flew by, and little drifting whorls of mist rose from the remaining banks of snow deep in the woods. Then suddenly there was the familiar voice raised in wild yelping somewhere among the dead cattails. And then a frantic surge of wings and old greenhead lifted out of the reeds, his mate behind him. They circled heavily while, unseen beneath them, Mutt plunged among the tangled reeds and knew a fragment of the ecstasy that had been his when guns had spoken over other ponds in other years.

I rose and ambled on until I found his tracks again, beyond the reeds. The trail led to the tamarack swamp and I saw where he had stopped a moment to snuffle at the still-unopened door of a chipmunk's burrow. Nearby there was a cedar tangle and the tracks went round and round beneath the boughs where a ruffed grouse had spent the night.

We crossed the clearing, Mutt and I, and here the soft black mold was churned and tossed as if by a herd of rutting deer; yet all the tracks were his. For an instant I was baffled, and then a butterfly came through the clearing on unsteady wings, and I remembered. So many times I had watched him leap and hop, and circle after such a one, forever led and mocked by the first spring butterflies.

STRAW HAT

I keep a prop and costume box
and this old straw hat has
turned up in a lot of paintings.
Backgrounds come from
everywhere — this weathered
old barn was in Southern
Alberta but the model posed for
the painting in my back garden.

OLD FRIENDS

(right) Like Farley Mowat in
April Passage, I suddenly
realized that the years had sped
by and my dog, Taffy, was
getting old. Everywhere I went
she came along and if I stopped
she urged me to continue the
walk. She'd posed for me since
she was a puppy. This was the
last painting I did of her.

Spring Breakup
Paul St. Pierre

Alexis Creek — All who love dirt roads and cheap whisky will want to note the most thrilling festival of the British Columbia interior which is called Spring Breakup. There is nothing in our cities to compare with it.

There are participants of the Spring Breakup jamboree kneeling beside the festival shrine — the boghole — stuffing wood under spinning truck wheels, soaking their suits in mud, and calling loudly upon their Maker in tones of deep emotion.

Nature arranges few things for men more colourful, invigorating, and exciting than breakup.

Breakup takes a lot of preparation which Nature, in her methodical manner, does all through the long winters in the Cariboo, Chilcotin, the Peace — anywhere that there are people to be inconvenienced.

Through winter's freezes and thaws, ice crystals form in the beds of roads. Sometimes they form a great lens of ice which remains invisible to the motorist as he speeds over it in those frozen months when the road surface may be as hard and smooth as pavement.

Then comes the thaw, and sometimes rain with it and, where once was a road, there remains naught but a dismal tarn ripped by ruts two feet deep and filled with brown water rimmed with shell ice.

These bogholes appear in low sections of the road or where culverts have plugged. They also appear in high sections of the road where no culverts have plugged. Nature works in mysterious ways.

They have a custom of appearing year after year, in the same section of road. This is handy for the highways people because they can tell, year after year, which sections of the road will cause complaint. They are thereby protected from unsettling surprises.

One boghole of memory in Chilcotin was one mile long and ran straight and true between rows of black jackpine beside some little lakes named the Crazy Lakes.

The local residents were wont to petition for culverts and for gravelling. After a few years they petitioned for a bridge or, failing that, ferry boats.

The government eventually rebuilt this road and the locals have had to take their complaints elsewhere, but this was, in a way, a pity, for the boghole was suited for a national shrine to the muffler and tailpipe industry.

I am no expert on bogholes, having never been stuck for longer than twelve consecutive hours in any one hole. Also, my experience is intermittent. I haven't been bogged down since the day before yesterday at North

BUCKAROO

(overleaf) The word "buckaroo," comes from the Spanish vaquero. For the annual rodeo in Jordan Valley, Idaho, the contestants come from miles around, dressed in their finest old-fashioned cowboy gear. They are hard working cowboys who look forward to this social occasion after many lonely months out on the plains.

Bend in the Fraser Canyon and it may not happen again for weeks. Some people get stuck every day at this time of year.

What can one do about bogholes?

Short of staying home, a cowardly course which our highways department recommends, one should pack a shovel, hip waders, chains, ropes and pulleys, an axe, a truck jack, food, tent, sleeping bag, and the Bible.

As you approach the boghole stop and look at it. Awful, isn't it?

There are chunks of wood floating in the puddles which appear to be the wreckage of rafts on which some poor wretches have tried to make it to shore. They aren't rafts. Wayfarers before you have jacked up the back wheels, poked boughs and logs underneath, and because they were lazy and laid the wood lengthwise, slipped off and bedded their car even deeper.

They should have laid the wood crossways for a corduroy road, as did their ancestors. Then twenty or thirty vehicles might have crossed this stretch before the corduroy sticks broke up, snatched off the muffler, and released the full-throated roar of the engine to the spring air.

Now having looked at the boghole and thought these thoughts, you should put on the waders and walk into the thing, testing for bottom which is there somewhere. In the overlay you will frequently discover big sharp rocks which can punch a hole in your oil pan and a bit of blood where the careless folk have cut themselves on ice or tire chains.

In the most famous of Chilcotin bogholes the mud has a rare consistency, and the natives call it the Fragrant Guano of the Great Northern Loon, Sweet Songstress of the Lonely Lakes, although they usually shorten the title.

By choosing your best rut, by rearranging any rocks, lunchpails, shovel heads, or other things you may find that won't float away, by chaining up the car before you get into trouble, you may make it to the other side where the road is merely sloppy and miserable.

Will you do that?

Of course not.

You will charge in, half way through the car will slow, give a gentle sigh, and come to rest high-centred and immovable.

Now you know why you brought the Bible.

Lengthening Shadows
W. O. Mitchell

Two days later, Brian lay under the hedge on the Sherry side of the house, his puppy in his arms. Sun streamed through the chinks in the Caragana leaves; a light breeze stirred them; Brian could see part of the road in front of the house; he could see two butterflies in lifting falling flight over the lawn patched with shade, briefly together, briefly apart. He lost sight of them by the spirea at the veranda.

The puppy whimpered slightly in its sleep; it nudged its head further into Brian's neck. The boy was aware that the yard was not still. Every grass-blade and leaf and flower seemed to be breathing, or perhaps whispering — something to him — something for him. The puppy's ear was inside out. Within himself, Brian felt a soft explosion of feeling. It was one of completion and of culmination.

The poplars along the road shook light from their leaves. A tin can rolled in the street; a newspaper plastered itself against the base of a telephone pole; loose dust lifted. Dancing down the road appeared a dust-devil. It stopped, took up again, and went whirling out to the prairie.

In the summer sky there, stark blue, a lonely goshawk hung. It drifted low in lazing circles. A pause — one swoop — galvanic death to a tan burgher no more to sit amid his city's grained heaps and squeak a question to the wind.

Shadows lengthen; the sunlight fades from cloud to cloud, kindling their torn edges as it dies from softness to softness down the prairie sky. A lone farmhouse window briefly blazes; the prairie bathes in mellower, yellower light, and the sinking sun becomes a low and golden glowing on the prairie's edge.

Leaning slightly backward against the reins looped around his waist, a man walks homeward from the fields. The horses' heads move gently up and down; their hoofs drop tired sounds, the jingle of the traces swinging at their sides is clear against the evening hush. The stubble crackles; a killdeer calls. Stooks, fences, horses, men have a clarity that was not theirs throughout the day.

Farm Friends
Robert Collins

My friends included a dog or two, and sinewy country cats named Greynose or Tabby, gliding like shadows along their beat — house to trees to barn to haystack checking for milk, scraps, mice and trouble. There were always round-eyed, cud-chewing cows, one named Reddy and another named Whiteface.

There were horses with distinct personalities. Old Jack was dean-of-men, a horse of infinite goodwill, who never flattened his ears in anger and always pulled his share of a load even when younger horses shirked. All he asked was kind words, oat sheaves, Sundays off and the occasional fresh, juicy corncob which, before munching, he rolled in his mouth like a Havana cigar. Tommy, the perennial teenager, was all muscle and feet with a roguish eye and a black velvet nose. Pat, the dappled grey, lean and peevish, would bite or kick me out of spite unless he wanted a favor. May — white, stubby, plodding, uncomplaining — reminded me of certain neighborhood housewives.

My associates included several hundred Barred Plymouth Rocks with red combs, shiny button eyes and rock bottom IQs. They lurked stupidly under the horses' feet, looking for fresh manure with grain in it. Horses were always stepping on them. Then the chicken mob,

like human and animal mobs since time began, tried to peck the cripples to death. My brother and I rescued and nursed them to health in a private compound known as the Chicken Hospital.

One invalid became a pet. He loved us to the bottom of his chicken heart and followed us everywhere, galumphing along on his gimpy leg, muttering affection from deep in his throat. It sounded like "Kuck" so we called him that. Having a pet chicken was weird enough; a pet chicken with a name that could be turned into an obscenity was social suicide.

One day my friend Roy Bien came by. He was four years older, a handsome, precocious, good-natured extrovert — everything that I was not. He played the guitar and yodelled like Wilf Carter. He knew the latest dirty jokes. Girls liked him. He could dance. He was allowed to work in the fields, a symbol of manhood. I would have crawled over hot coals — no, I would have *gone down in the cellar* — to win his approval.

Now he said, "That's a funny-looking chicken."

"That's Kuck," said my brother, too young to understand the value of lying.

"That's WHAT?" whooped Roy Bien, sensing a bit of madness that would convulse our school friends for

NEW COLT

(left) Children everywhere seem to have a fascination for the newly born. Perhaps they feel a special relationship with the youngsters of the animal kingdom. In the country they are close to the start of new lives but they never lose their sense of awe and wonder.

BABY CHICKS

(right) I was attracted to the striking contrast of light and dark in a warm shed where some baby chicks had recently been hatched. There's that old straw hat again, catching the light from an unseen window.

LGRIBBS

weeks to come. In one-tenth of a second I had to choose between losing Roy Bien's favor or selling out in front of my brother.

"Uh . . . we call it . . . uh . . . *Cluck*," I mumbled apologetically. "Because it makes that . . . uh . . . funny clucking noise. Y'know?"

"Oh yeah, Cluck," said Roy Bien, immediately bored.

My brother looked strangely at Kuck and me, wondering which was the chicken, but kept his silence and let me save face.

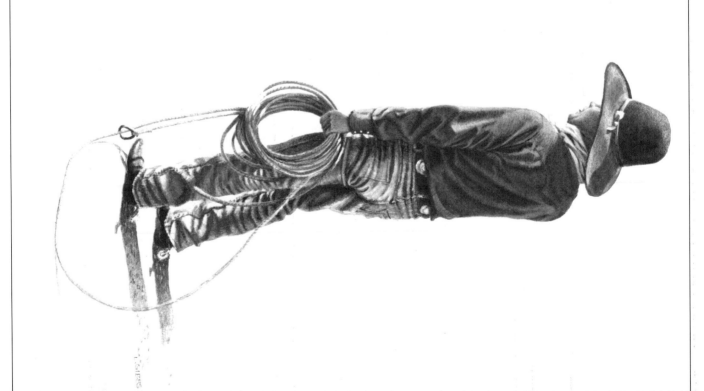

Long, Long Nights

The Ghostly Dance

Morley Callaghan

Why in Regina, come to think of it, it often didn't seem to be cold at all. It's the dry air, so crisp and exhilarating. One night when it was twenty-five below zero I was walking along blithely with a friend, feeling light and lively, with the northern lights winging overhead as if a giant ribbon counter had been caught in an electric fan. When we passed under a street light my western friend said casually, "You better watch that ear. I think it's turning white." Hands over my ears I headed for the nearest restaurant.

I think of that frost-bitten ear now, seeing it in my mind against the prairie wheat fields just before harvest time when you are looking across a flat land for miles and miles from some high office building or hotel room, and this land with its ripening wheat is one big warm golden bowl in the sunlight. The contrast! The frozen ear, the warm glowing bowl. It's Canada. And just a few months later this golden carpet, when winter settles in, becomes an endless howling winter desert, and those unpainted farm houses look bleak, cold and lonely against the wild winter extravagance of the northern lights. Then a sense of isolation literally reaches through the train window at you. It's winter loneliness. It's not like the summer prairie loneliness that has a touch of pleasurable

melancholy to it when the moon rises and a dog barks and the land and the sky seem to come closer together in stillness and evenness: no grandeur, nothing wild. It is something of a prairie winter wildness that I always remember.

One February afternoon on a train crossing the prairies in a blizzard the man who was sitting across from me, a westerner, friendly and loquacious, banged my knee. "Look, there they are," he said, "What did I tell you," and I looked out.

The blizzard snow, coming in whirling patches, made a shifting cold gray screen against the window; then would come sudden clear patches that seemed to have endless depths til they too were screened. The man had been telling me that wild horses still roamed the prairie. I had never quite believed in these horses. But there, now, out there in the blizzard about a quarter of a mile away a herd of horses came charging along. Sometimes screened off, they became part of the blizzard.

Sometimes they came into one of the clear patches as they raced along, ghost horses, tossing their heads, all white in the swirling snow, and I watched them raptly as if I suspected they were trying to tell me something with their ghostly dance.

LATE RUN

(right) Swift and sturdy wild horses still roam the plains and foothills of the west. They break down fences, which makes them unpopular with ranchers, but these men will tell you, you can ruin a good horse trying to capture one of these mustangs.

Something Wonderful
Andy Russell

The days were a blur of unending cold, tired muscles, creaking hooves and sleigh runners, and the steamy smell of horses. One night the thermometer dropped to fifty-two below, but it didn't seem to be much colder when I went out next morning.

On the way to the haystack old Phil told me, "Your nose is freezing. You'd better thaw it out with your hand." I took a look at him to see that his beaky nose was white as bone. "Yours is froze solid," I told him. He felt it gingerly and cussed, "Damn if it ain't! Hard enough to peck holes in a board!"

I couldn't help laughing and he looked hard at me with sharp blue eyes past the hand that was holding his nose, in a way that shut me up. Then he chuckled and remarked, "We can still laugh anyway. Things could be worse."

Like almost every boy in the country, I had aspirations to become a cowboy, but this part of it I could do without. There seemed to be no end to the cold. Dad was up and around again, but too weak to do very much, I couldn't remember what it was like not to be tired.

Then one evening just as we were finishing supper, the house suddenly cracked. Dad went to the door and looked out. "It's a chinook!" he exclaimed. "It feels

warm as summer!" Next morning it was forty above and water was dripping from the leaves. The temperature had risen about eighty degrees in fourteen hours. In three days the hills were bare on the south slopes and the stock was lazing about enjoying the warmth. The wind continued to blow soft and warm, and apart from a few short snow storms the back of the winter had been broken.

Winter weather in wintertime is one thing, but when cold and snow hold on stubbornly into spring and the calving season, the life of a cowman can be tough. In the old days on the open range the cows were pretty much alone when it came to calving. If one got into trouble and was lucky enough to be spotted in time, she got help, but much more often she was on her own. It was a stark matter of survival of the fittest. Consequently, genetics had arranged that they didn't have trouble nearly as often as the more pampered cattle of today. Vets were few and far between and such things as caesarean operations were unknown. It is amazing what a cow can stand and even more impressive how newborn calves manage to survive, though there is a preponderance of bobbed tails and cropped ears from being frozen in a bad spring.

I remember a miserable night twenty-odd years ago, when our phone rang at midnight and a neighbor was on the line. One of his heifers was in trouble calving and, would I give him a hand? I put on some warm clothes and tied on my snowshoes, for the roads were blocked by drifts. When I arrived at his place, it was to find him out among his cattle with his Land Rover. The heifer had a calf stuck in her pelvic opening with its front feet showing, and she was so spooky that he couldn't get her into the barn. A good-looking, strong Aberdeen Angus, she was in no mood to be pushed around. While I watched she lay down and heaved on the calf, but it was being just as stubborn as its mother and didn't budge.

I got a lariat and a short piece of sashcord, then sat on the hood of the vehicle, while my friend eased it up to the heifer. She jumped up and started to move off, but I got a loop over her head and snubbed her to the bumper of the truck.

Closer examination showed the calve's head was where it should be, so I looped the sash cord over its feet like short hobbles and pulled. Seeming to realize that I wanted to help, the heifer lay down. Sitting down and bracing my feet against her rump, I timed my pulls with her heaves and in a few moments the calf was out in the snow. I picked it up and put it on some dry straw, then turned its mother loose. While we watched, she went to it and began to lick it vigorously and before long it was up on wobbly legs and busy sucking a bellyful of warm milk.

Even there in the dark with snow spitting on the wind there was something wonderful about it — an inert, wet, little thing suddenly blossoming into life and responding to its mother's care. The tired lines of my friend's face softened and smoothed out as he watched. "He'll make it now," he said. "Let's go have a drink. I got a bottle of Old Stump Blower for times like this."

SADDLE

(overleaf, left) The western saddle is big and comfortable, a practical design for those who spend long hours on a horse. It has a high cantle at the back to keep the rider from slipping off as he works with a balky steer. It is really the cowhand's "office" with a saddle horn to hold the rope, tie downs to hold rain gear, perhaps a saddle bag for miscellaneous equipment.

PASSING

(overleaf, right) Both the building and the traditional cowboy are passing into another era. As steel barns replace wood structures, and jeeps, trail bikes and helicopters replace the cowboy's horse, I sought to capture a timeless quality with the two of them still together.

Tell Me about the Winters

Morley Callaghan

If you said tell me about the winters, I'd say what do I know about winter, I have seen too many of them, they have been with me too long, they are part of my life, I cannot separate myself from them, nor would I want to. Though I have said cynically many times that this country was founded on the glowing big-bellied stove and should have on the national flag not the maple leaf but the Quebec heater, and though some of my neighbors now will be preparing for the annual escape to the Bahamas, I am here where I was born, getting some kind of quiet pleasure watching the city get snowed in on this mild winter night. I always feel younger on such a night, especially if the moon comes out after it has stopped snowing.

My father used to smile and say that Kipling had called Canada Our Lady of the Snows, and the smile was like a wink, warning me that Kipling knew nothing about Canada. But a little Canadian kid doesn't know that there are strange lands where there is no snow. When you are very young you love the winter. A child comes along the street crying and shivering, his wet-mitted hands lifeless at his sides, his neck red from his wet scarf, and his feet soaking wet. But as soon as he gets home and has his mitts placed on the hot radiator, and his socks changed

and pants dried, he rushes out again. As soon as he learns to walk he is given a sleigh for Christmas, or a toboggan and taken to some hill or park. If his father says he is too young for skis he makes them out of barrel staves with strips of leather nailed on them as hooks for your feet, and even before he can skate he is playing hockey on the street, or on a hose-frozen rink in his backyard. And if, as he grows older, he hears some teacher refer to the winter as "the great Canadian challenge," he thinks the man is crazy.

Kids use the winter. They play with it. Winter happiness in Canada seems to come to those who know how to use this season. Some even use it in a weird way for a satisfaction they can't get at any other time of year.

The Young Ones

L.GIBBS

RED SHOES

(left) One of those happy paintings that came about quite by accident. This child was posing for another painting when her feet got cold in the water she warmed them in the soft sand.

HIPPITY HOPS

The great excitement in a rural community is the annual picnic. The sack race was always a popular event, even though the sacks today are plastic grain bags. The fun is ageless. One of the little girls is going to fall down giggling before she finishes the race.

Summer Games
Fredelle Bruser Maynard

Summer in Birch Hills was the lovely season. It was what we waited for, all through the long months when dark came early and the cold shut us indoors by the throbbing stove. May Day brought promise; we raced from door to door with crepe paper candy baskets. Then Victoria Day; we paraded in middies and gym bloomers celebrating, not a long dead queen, but liberation to come. And on the last day of June we burst out of the school doors with wild cries of delight.

> *No more pencils, no more books,*
> *No more teacher's dirty looks!*

On the first of July, whirling our fizzy sparklers or lighting Roman candles that jetted in the velvet dark, we knew that we were immortal and that summer would never end.

At first no day was long enough for all we had to do, Fern and Hazel and I. There was the playhouse to clean up. We stamped the dirt floor till it was smooth as linoleum, scrubbed the shelves and set out the doll dishes. We took down last year's faded brown pictures and tacked up new ones clipped from magazines and old calendars. Sometimes we skipped through the back lanes checking trash barrels for useful oddments, but we gave that up after Fern got a bad cut from the jagged edge of an old tin can. Mud pies, daisy chains, hopscotch, choke-cherries . . . the days flew past. By the middle of August, we were

seized with a curious mixture of restlessness and boredom. When you came right down to it, what was there really, to do?

We branched out. "Let's collect rocks," Hazel would say. Or butterflies, or chips of colored glass. For a while we would be fired with competitive excitement. But then, when the coffee cans were full of specimens, the game died. "I've got an idea," Hazel said one day. "We can study bugs."

I rolled over, sucking the moist root of a grass blade. "Who wants to *study* anything?"

Summer evenings so far north were late bright. You could race out after supper any night and find a gang ready to play. In the brief democracy of those waning hours, children of all ages joined in; it was the best moment for team games. That is how I see Birch Hills now, in dusky lavender light. We have gathered in a field by the skating rink; the town lies behind us, the woods thicken round. I smell crushed grass and clover and — from a nearby garden, heavy, sickish-sweet — the white night-blooming tobacco plant. Fireflies wink and fade. Someone calls, "Run! Quick!" All the others have made it, across a dangerous no-man's land to the safety of goal, and in the sudden dark I hear the leader's cry:

> *Red Rover, Red Rover,*
> *I call Fredelle over.*

The Hero
Oren Robison

Just as inevitably as grain ripens, equipment breaks down during harvest — especially, it seems, when all other conditions are perfect.

The seven-year-old boy had no idea that his incessant chatter was compounding the frustrations of the two men as they struggled to repair the machine.

In the boy's eyes Uncle Lloyd was a hero. The breakdown represented nothing more than a chance to talk and be near him.

The hired man, clanking his wrenches and muttering under his breath was just an audience — and not a very attentive one at that.

Uncle Lloyd leaned back from his work. Taking a rag from the back pocket of his coveralls, he wiped the grease from his hands.

He squinted at the sun and mused that it "must be getting on to milking time."

"Somebody ought to be bringing the cows in from pasture," he said. "I've got to get to get this machine running— think you could bring the cows in for me, boy?"

The kid's heart soared at the chance to do something so important; but silent wails of fear shrilled through his mind. He was afraid of cows, except when Uncle Lloyd was near.

He was a town kid, after all, just visiting the farm. But a man of seven could never let on that he was "chicken."

The kid started along the winding path to the pasture, a quarter mile distant. Out of his uncle's sight, he stopped. He couldn't make himself go on but he had no excuse not to. He couldn't go back and tell Uncle Lloyd he was afraid.

Then he remembered that his nine-year-old sister was up at the house. Even having a girl with him would be better than going alone — but his uncle mustn't see, for if he did, he'd guess the reason.

With all the craftiness learned from the John Wayne Saturday matinees, he crept behind the machine shed, made a dash by the pig pen; a quick sprint to the chicken coop; belly down through the grass to the summer kitchen; then he was at the house.

"He asked you to do it, so get going — or are ya chicken?" She was scared of cows too, but being nine, she'd never admit it.

What'd she have to go and say that for? He wanted to give her pigtail a yank, but that would definitely mean going to the pasture alone.

She agreed to go with him when he promised to

THE VISITOR

I couldn't resist this pink skinned little city boy contrasted against the weathered old farmer. The representation of flight from the model airplane in the boy's hands is picked up again with the flight of birds over the granaries in the background.

show her a flicker woodpecker's nest in the big, dead tree near the pasture.

Together they sneaked back around the outbuildings. They were committed now. The enormity of shared dread stopped them in their tracks.

They picked up the biggest sticks in sight. You never know when you might have to club some crazed brute into submission in the middle of a stampede.

Holding hands and brandishing their clubs, babbling mindless reassurances to each other, they advanced warily into the face of bovine danger.

Halfway to the pasture they had to step aside for a Holstein, coming toward them with the ponderous, determined shuffle of one who knows it's milking time and intends to be punctual.

Behind her plodded the rest of the herd, docile, lowing with the urgency of getting to the barn.

The kids watched wide-eyed as the great brutes passed.

Bravado returned. Cows weren't as dumb as they looked. Somehow they had sensed that with herdsmen of such great skill and courage, acting fractious would gain them nothing.

The clubs were dropped. Now that these dogies understood their place they were gittin' along just fine.

At the barn, each cow swayed into her own place and stood patiently, waiting to be given a ration of chop— and to be milked.

Outside, the roar of the engine was proof that repairs had finally been accomplished.

Feeling somewhat heroic himself now, the boy swaggered out, calling, "I brought the cows in for you, Uncle Lloyd!"

With all the condescension he could muster, he added that his sister had "tagged along."

A powerful hand gently ruffled the boy's hair, while over his head, Uncle Lloyd's wink and the hired man's knowing smile of reply passed unnoticed by the boy.

"Thanks boy. You'll never know what a big help you've been to me."

And to the boy, aglow in his hero's approval, there never was a more glorious autumn day.

Hallowe'en

Betty Gibbs

The old house was dark as we lined ourselves in front of the door and chorused hopefully; "Hallowe'en Apples!"

The echoes of our voices swirled around in darkness and lost themselves in silence.

"Hallowe'en Apples!"

Again, silence. Without a word we hoisted our encumbering skirts and turned to retrace our steps along the narrow, tree-lined path.

Behind us the knob turned and the door screeched open a few slow inches.

"Come in," said a dry, raspy voice that rustled like autumn leaves in the wind. "Come in my dears. I've been hoping some young people would come by."

Together we swung around, eyes wide like a tree full of owls. There was no one framed in the half open doorway.

"Come in," the voice rattled again.

Shoved rudely by one of my companions, I lurched first into the house. My friends shuffled in behind me. We were something right out of Macbeth, Katy and Fran and I, three black clad witches carrying pillow cases bulging with apples and candy.

In the closeness of the scant hall one flickering candle set in a human skull shed an uncertain light on a small table and an open book. Beyond, almost lost in the darkness, I thought I could see a basket of polished apples and a bowl of popcorn balls.

It was a joke! I knew it was a joke. I tried to find my voice and turned to smile my appreciation of this scary foolishness.

The door clicked shut. In the shadow beside it stood a plump evil witch. Mrs. Norman? It had to be. It looked a little like the lady we'd seen out raking leaves.

A little, but different — long, stringy white hair, a leering, malevolent smile; was Mrs. Norman really a witch? The same doubts were in Katy's mind. Her sweaty fingers clung tightly to mine.

In a cold congealing silence she contemplated us with scornful eyes. Fran found her voice first. She cleared her throat and with a forced heartiness she quavered, "Hi, Mrs. Norman."

The witch ignored her.

"Sign your name in blood," she cackled, holding out a quill pen and indicating the book on the table.

We bumped into one another in our eagerness to do as we were told.

Blood? Or red ink? We were beyond being sure.

In turn we wrote our names and turned to escape but the witch was standing in front of the door.

PUMPKIN

(overleaf, left) After Hallowe'en a brilliant patch of orange put color among the deep earthy tones of dead foliage and gave a touch of life and warmth to the ending season.

REHEARSING

(overleaf, right) Rather than paint actual performances I lean toward depicting the activity behind the scenes. The intense concentration of these two dancers as they waited backstage for their part of the rehearsal was more interesting than the actual performance.

"Entertain me!" she crowed.

We stopped still in stunned surprise. Entertain her! How, when our knees were already buckling with fright?

"Entertain me," she ordered again. "A little song, a pretty dance; do your best my dears. I have some interesting tortures if you fail to please me." Her wrinkled fingers closed on Katy's arm.

"Nice soup bone that," she nodded to herself.

"We could . . ." Fran stopped to clear her throat.

"We could sing a round."

A round. Good, I thought. We'd all be done at the same time.

 Three blind mice, three blind mice,
 They all ran after the farmer's wife
 Who cut off their tails with . . .

I wished that Fran had chosen a different song.

At last we were finished.

The witch said not a word but solemnly filled our bags with apples and popcorn balls. She opened the door for us.

"Tell no one what has happened here tonight. Come again," she cackled as we fled through the gate.

Tripping and stumbling we ran to the corner, called goodnight to each other and didn't stop running until we were safely inside our own homes.

We didn't tell anyone and we never went back; not even at Christmas when Mrs. Norman invited the neighborhood children in for cocoa and carol singing; not even on Valentine's Day when Mrs. Norman had spicy, heart-shaped cookies for everyone.

We never went back, for we were never sure who had received us that Hallowe'en.

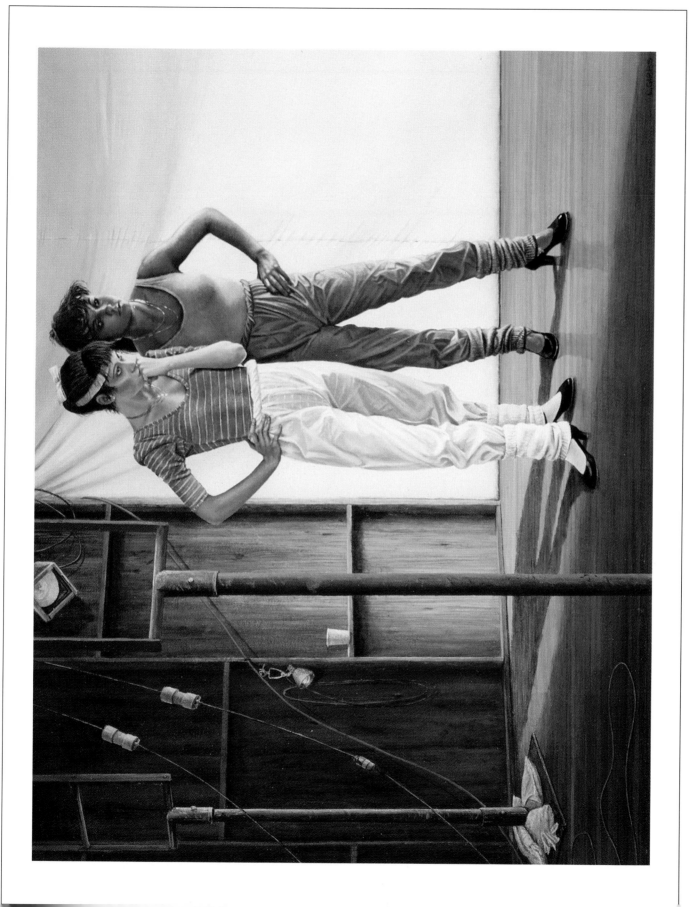

School Days
Peter Shostak

For me school was a wonderful place, where, through a small number of books, I was introduced to the world which went beyond our simple farming community. Through my reading Dick, Jane, Sally and Puff became new friends who lived in a city far away. Although I had no first-hand knowledge of their place of play and work, I accepted them and eagerly began to tackle the important task of learning to read and write.

In my case this proved to be more difficult than for most, as I could not speak or understand English. My knowledge of this foreign language was limited to a working vocabulary of two words — "yes" and "no."

Initially, the awe of the two-room schoolhouse with an entire row of Grade 1 pupils, and, most importantly, the realization that not everyone spoke and understood Ukrainian, especially my teacher Mrs. O'Connor, did present extra problems.

Our communication difficulties became evident when, on the first day, shortly after the classroom was organized into five rows of desks, roughly representing a different grade in each row, Mrs. O'Connor wrote several numbers on the blackboard and asked the first grade students if they knew what they were. My correct response to the number five was met by several suppressed giggles and a blank stare from my teacher. A Grade 4 student came to my rescue. After my enthusiastic response was shot down, and I had no way of knowing what to say or do, he explained in Ukrainian that I was to speak only in English. At least now, I knew what the problem was. Mrs. O'Connor and I did have communication difficulties but by Christmas I understood a great deal of what she was saying and by Easter she understood me. Humorous misunderstandings occurred when I grasped only one meaning of a word which had two or more distinct meanings. For example, the Grade 3 class kept repeating that a foot is always twelve inches long and I could not understand how this statement was true since after repeated measurements, I found that my feet were barely seven inches long.

The school concert was one of the social highlights and almost everyone was there, especially the families whose children were attending the school. It is hard to imagine how, clad in heavy winter clothes, they all fit into that small room. Little children were held by the parents as they patiently awaited the start of the concert. Some promptly fell asleep and did not awaken until the first round of applause filled the room, while others slept through the entire concert.

PICNIC AT THE LAKE

(overleaf) All dressed up in her finest, this little girl captured my imagination with her frilly little dress, the saggy socks and worn moccasins.

The red curtain hid from view the last minute stage preparations and adjustments. From the shuffling of feet and the whispering of children on the stage and the movement of the curtain one could only guess what was happening. For the young children and adults patiently waiting there were many false starts. By the time the curtain finally parted far enough to permit the teacher or one of the senior students, who assumed the role of master of ceremonies, to welcome everyone and introduce the first item of the program, the room was packed.

Generous and enthusiastic applause for the first group of performers awakened some of the sleeping children and frightened several others who, although awake, had difficulty determining what was happening. A recitation followed by a play, followed by another carol or two, were performed on the stage and after two hours the concert drew to a close.

Scars
W. P. Kinsella

It seems like an awful thing to say but it would have been better if it was one of the Bottle girls that died. Annie Bottle and about nine kids live poor as coyotes with a mean husband. Rebecca Snakeskin was Mary's only child.

The funeral be a bad scene too and after it for about three weeks Mary Snakeskin don't come out of her cabin. Everybody try to be nice to her but she hardly talk to anybody and when she do she blame them for kill her little girl. "Sad people say a lot more than they mean," say Mad Etta, and shrug her buffalo-big shoulders. "She'll come around."

After a while people go about their own business and leave Mary alone. Everybody got their own troubles.

Nobody paid any attention when it first started, but Jenny Bottle made some calls on Mrs. Snakeskin. I don't know why she done it, maybe just because she have a good heart. Jenny is I guess eight years old, skinny, with a pinched face, but tough as red willow. Her eyes is close together and her skin tight on her bones, not the least bit like Rebecca, who was short and round like her mama.

Jenny began to spend a lot of time with Mary Snakeskin and everybody who see what is happening say that it is a good thing. She stay overnight at Mary's cabin

and walk down to Hobbema General Store to buy groceries for her. When hockey season get going strong Mary go back to her job. Everybody is some happy for her. It is only then though, that people learn about the funny way she see the world. She all the time talk to the other ladies at the concession stand about her little girl Rebecca as though she was still alive, and one night when Jenny Bottle come to see her at work, Mary call her Rebecca, and talk to Jenny like she was her dead daughter.

Pretty soon Jenny start to live in with Mary full time. Jenny start to grow a little more meat on her bones and Mary buy her some warm clothes for the winter like she never had before.

Etta always like to keep a jump or two ahead of any trouble on the reserve so she take me along over to Annie Bottle's place one summer afternoon. Fred Bottle is off in jail for a month or so, so this be one of the better times for Annie. Her cabin smell of grease and mouldy things, and there be a whole bunch of kids sit around on a mattress that lay in the corner of the floor.

Annie wear a long skirt of a purple colour with lots of stains on it, and a kerchief tied tight over her head and knotted under her chin. She walk like an old woman and

42

all the time look at the ground.

Etta talk about small things, look at a couple of kids that Annie say been sick and say she'll bring over some stuff to cure their ringworm.

"So what do you hear from Jenny?" she finally say.

Annie mumble something in Cree that I can't make out. She raise up her eyes that are tiny and dull. "I'm glad she got a better place," she say.

Annie got a bad scar from her ear to the corner of her nose on the left side. I hear tell that Frank Bottle bust a plate over her face one time when he was drunk. Annie look like people been beating on her all her life. Seeing Annie Bottle live the way she do is the reason I believe in a heaven of some kind. There got to be a better place than Hobbema for people like Annie after they die.

"I'm glad she got a better place," is the only words Annie speak of her daughter.

On the way back Etta say, "So who's it doing any harm to? Little Rebecca's dead, but if Mary want to get a new kid to take her place, and call *her* Rebecca, then what's the harm?"

"Hey, I'm your assistant remember? You don't have to convince me. It white peoples who think that what's going on is funny."

"Most everything in the world is funny if you look at it from the right angle," Etta say. Seem to me everybody be getting along okay and they stay that way unless the white peoples come along to mess it up. Etta, I guess, know that it just be a matter of time. It be just a month or so later that Mary Snakeskin try to register Jenny in the Grade Three class.

Mary pretend that Miss Waits don't bother her none. Guess maybe it ain't pretend. Mary's face is clear and round, so smooth and shiny it could be waxed like the hardwood floor at Blue Quills Hall.

Her and Jenny go everywhere together. It is pretty easy to tell by the look on her face that what Mary see when she look at Jenny Bottle is not the frail-shouldered little girl in front of her, but her own dead daughter who liked to dance in front of people and had a laugh as bright as sunlight on the water.

What we like to do is keep Indian Affairs Department far away from this whole scene. Wouldn't matter a bit to them if Mary and Jenny was happy or not. What they worry about is all the rules they got written down in black books in their offices. Indians might as well be cords of stove wood the way that the government figure.

Talk around the reserve is that if Indian Affairs get involved they take Jenny away from Mary Snakeskin, get a judge to say that Jenny have to go in a home for kids some place away from the reserve, and maybe Mary have to go in the place for crazy people at Ponoka.

"I think it about time we walk up there to the school and talk with Miss Waits," say Etta. It got to be a mile or more up to the school and what Etta mean by walk is from her cabin to Blind Louis Coyote's pickup truck which she expect me to borrow and also get some friends to help load and unload her. I get the truck and my friends Frank Fencepost and Rufus Firstrider, put a chair up in the back, then one pull while two of us push Mad Etta up the door from Onewound's outhouse which is what we always got to use for a ramp.

"What do you figure makes Mary the way she is?" I ask.

"Grief have different effect on different people," Etta say. "Some people show their scars, some cover them up and on some people scars don't take."

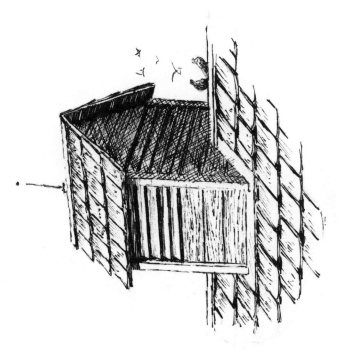

"I remember once after a thunderstorm," I say, "me and Illianna and Joseph, we went outside and picked up damp rose petals. We stuck them on our faces and they dried there. Look like scars." But it don't seem to me that Etta is listening.

"If you was a medicine man, Silas, how would you handle this?" Etta say to me as we tramp up the long path to the teacher's apartment block of the Residential School.

"I tell the truth. I tell Miss Waits how what happen makes Mary a happy person again and how Jenny got a better home than she ever had before, and how it is a kind of make-believe that hurt no-one."

"How you think that go over with Miss Waits?"

"White people don't take no stock in make-believe. They'd have to fill out Government forms before they could have a vision."

HER SMALL CORNER

This youngster has posed for me many times. At the beginning of summer holidays she had braces and had just had her hair cut short. She was going through a time of not liking herself much, so while her friends romped on the beach she found a secluded place to make "cookies" for her dad.

Down Home

Practical Jokes
Max Braithwaite

If it were a Sunday, the farmer would show me around his place and maybe play a practical joke. All rural folk are great hands at practical jokes, and my farmers were no exception. And once a good one had been got off, it became part of the folklore of the district.

There was the time, for instance, that Sandy Sanderson instructed a greenhorn from the East in the art of harnessing a team of horses, and then gave him a mare and a stud to harness together. The joke came off well; the greenhorn suffered two broken ribs and a mild concussion.

Or the time Wilbur Burke disguised his voice and phoned from Saskatoon to tell the young female teacher that the inspector would be there Monday. And of course all the school kids were in on it and got a great charge out of watching her fuss and fret and get ready for somebody they knew wouldn't be there for months. This one wasn't a complete success however, because nobody was hurt.

The one of which I was a victim came close to being a classic; I almost got killed. I was visiting Leo Ryan, a round faced Irishman who raised Aberdeen Angus cattle. He took me into the pasture to see some choice steers, but one of them turned out to be a bull.

"Gawdamighty!" Leo breathed from behind me. "I didn't know that old brute was loose. Watch out, he's a mean one!"

The bull was about a hundred feet from us. It raised its head, stared in our direction and sniffed the air.

"Will he come after us?" I asked. And I was scared.

"Not if we don't run. Don't let him see you're scared. Keep your eye on him and back slowly towards the fence. Mind . . . don't make any sudden moves. He won't chase you if you don't run." This was good advice, I'm sure, but somehow the bull got his wires crossed. For although I backed away at a snail's pace and kept my eyes fastened on his, he began to come for me first at a walk, then at a trot.

"What will I do?" I hissed over my shoulder.

"Run like hell!" came the shouted instructions from back at the fence. As soon as Leo had told me about not running he'd beat it for the fence as fast as he could go, which naturally had upset the bull.

I made it to the fence, but with little dignity or aplomb.

The story got a big laugh at dinner and later around the district. To this day I'll wager any wag can bring down the house simply by screwing up his face and shouting, "Run like hell!"

Heart of a Lifestyle
Jayne Heese

Today as yesterday on the Canadian prairies, one room remains the centre of life. It is in the kitchen — over strong coffee — that business is conducted, strategies are planned, and entertaining is done. The front door of most rural homes opens straight into this heart of the rural lifestyle. Those who venture in are usually content to venture no further than the kitchen table whether they come on business or personal matters. Work in progress — baking, canning or pickling, can be continued throughout conversation and the inevitable cups of coffee.

In recent years many of the old farmstead homes have been replaced or rebuilt, but the importance of that special space and the multiple roles it plays has never been lost. The small galley and adjoining dining room of the city house is not incorporated into the design of a new farm home. Indeed, a living room may be decreased in size or a separating wall deleted to allow for more kitchen area, all the better to accommodate the array of articles which may be found there.

Amid an air of organized confusion, the kitchen serves equally well as a laboratory, office, mess hall and conference room. It has not been unknown for that same utilitarian room to serve as a veterinary clinic or plant nursery. A warmed oven may revive a shivering newborn orphan. Sunny windowsills may be nurturing potted seedlings. One cupboard drawer may be given to storing wayward mechanic's tools rather than kitchen gadgets, and during harvest time, the table's centrepiece may make way for a grain moisture testing device. A microwave oven may well share a shelf with a citizen's band radio which provides a link with mobile members of the family.

The electronic media has its own place in the contemporary farm kitchen. Handy to the table — so that the latest agricultural news can be digested while the noon meal is eaten — can be found a television set, and likely a radio. A pen and paper, or perhaps a computer close at hand means grain and stock prices can be recorded as they are broadcast.

Integral to this keeping track of the world around a prairie farm is a simple device — large and strategically placed windows invariably provide good views from both the table and the kitchen sink. The drapes are not drawn day or night. Only on the hottest of summer days will a blind be drawn, blocking the view of sky and countryside. The kitchen is the farmer's lookout on the world. Voracious consumers and hoarders of information, they turn to print as well as vocal and visual gathering

THE LONG WATCH

Men of the saddle can be just as comfortable on a horse as they are in a rocking chair. Scattered pockets of cattle have to be re-joined to the main herd. This cattle man in Southern Alberta was just taking a few minutes to relax before he started to move them.

methods. Thus this room becomes a resource centre of agriculturally-oriented publications. Even the calendar, which never fails to hang on the wall by the phone, is a wealth of information in itself — a detailed diary of daily occurences, from who stopped in that day and how much a tonne of grain was selling for, to precipitation readings and a record of acres worked.

Ultimately the farm kitchen becomes a universal room. The family gathers there each morning, noon and night. The day's activities are planned beforehand and analysed after. Through all the comings and goings of the day, that central revolving point remains constant. And when the last light is shut off for the night, that same bulb, the one in the kitchen, will be the first one lit in the morning.

Worn Horseshoes
Louis Bromfield

I t was a big red barn built in the days when farmers were rich and took pride in their barns. Ohio is filled with these barns which are an expression of everything that is good in farming, barns in which their owners took great pride. Nowadays one sees often enough great new barns on dairy farms owned by great corporations, or stock farms owned by millionaires; but these new barns have no character. They express nothing but utility and mechanized equipment, with no soul, no beauty, no individuality. Already they appear on any country landscape, commonplace and standardized without beauty or individuality — in fifty years they will simply be eyesores.

The old barns built in a time of the great tradition of American agriculture when the new land was still rich and unravaged by greed and bad farming, had each one its own character, its special beauty born of the same order of spirit and devotion which built the great cathedrals of Chartres or Rheims or Salzburg. They were built out of love and pride in the earth, each with a little element of triumphal boastfulness — as if each barn was saying to all the rich neighboring countryside, "Look at me! What a fine splendid thing I am, built by a loving master, sheltering fat cattle and big uddered cows and great bins

of grain! Look at me! A temple to plenty and to the beauty of the earth! A temple of abundance and good living!"

And, they were not built *en série*, like barracks. Each rich farmer had his own ideas, bizarre sometimes, fanciful with fretwork and cupolas and big handsome paintings of a Belgian stallion or a shorthorn bull, the main cupola bearing a pair of trotting horses, bright with gilt, as a weathervane. They were barns with great, cavernous mows filled with clover hay, two stories or three in height, with the cattle and horses below bedded in winter in clean straw, halfway to their fat bellies. Perhaps there was waste space or they were inconveniently planned for doing the chores, but there was a splendor and nobility about them which no modern hip-roofed, standardized monstrosity can approach. Ohio is filled with them — Gothic barns, Pennsylvania Dutch barns with stone pillars, New England barns attached to the house itself, the stone ended barns of Virginia and even baroque barns. There is in Ohio no regional pattern of architecture as there is in New England or the Pennsylvania Dutch county. Ohio was settled by people from all the coastal states each bringing his own tradition with him and so there is immense variety.

BY THE FORGE

(overleaf, left) Dark interiors and bright contrasts always interest me. I like the old stump, being used for an anvil, that looks as though it's been there forever, and the accumulation of clutter on the floor.

REFIT

Every boy who lives near water would like to have a boat of his own. In this case, his father said, "You want it, you paint it." His clean jeans didn't stay that way for long, but eventually he finished painting the boat, and about half the dock.

In my boyhood all these barns had a rich, well-painted appearance. Those owned by farmers with an ancient Moravian background outdid the barns which only had a single stallion or bull painted on them; they had painted on the big sliding barn door a whole farm landscape for which the farm itself had served as a model and in it appeared bulls and cows, calves and stallions, hens and ducks and guinea fowls, horses and sheep and hogs. They were hex paintings and their roots lay, not in Ohio or even in the coastal states, but far back in the darkness of medieval Germany, in a world of bald mountains and *Walpurgisnächte*. They were painted there on the big barn doors as a safeguard against the spells of witches, against vampires and incubi, for it was believed and it is still believed among the old people, that a spell cast by any malicious neighboring witch on the cattle in one of these great barns would fall not on the cattle themselves but upon the representations painted on the barn door. Always they were painted artlessly by someone on the farm and some of them had a fine primitive quality of directness and simplicity of conception.

Usually over the doors of these painted barns there hung a worn horseshoe, for it was believed that the witches had an overweening passion for mathematics coupled with a devouring curiosity. If a witch sought during the night to sweep through the barn door on her broomstick and found herself confronted by a used horseshoe, she was forced to turn about and have no peace until she had retraced and counted all the hoofprints made by the shoe. The more worn the shoe the better, for it would take her all the longer to satisfy her compulsion, and she would not have completed her impossible task before morning arrived and she had to return whence she came. If the shoe had been worn long enough the prints it had made would be so numerous that she could never count them all in a single night. As each night she had to begin afresh, she would never be able, even in the long nights of winter, to get through the door to do evil to the cattle.

L.GIBBS

53

The Wilderness Men

L GIBS

MORNING RIDE

Up on a cold morning and into the saddle by dawn, these men will not find warmth and comfort again before nightfall.

WINTER COATS

Nature covers everything with a warm blanket of snow, the horse grows a winter coat, the man protects his face with a beard. Both belong in the wilderness. Night will fall soon but they are not far from the warmth of the cabin. The angles of their heads are reechoed in the shapes of the rocks.

A Two Years Cub
Sid Marty

Every night at 10 o'clock
just when I'm nicely dozing off
he climbs my porch
and cuffs with a snort
and a clatter
the white enamel washbasin
like a saucer through the moonlight
yards out into the meadow

I'll be damned if I move that basin
just because it's sitting
on his ancestral trail
bisected by this ancient shack

Listen pup
there's another porch
ten miles up the valley
Why single my sleep out for murder?

Don't laugh!
You come back tomorrow night
gonna boot you up the ass

It's quiet for awhile
I settle down, mollified

Only to shoot up in wild eyed terror
Sounds like a steam engine
nosing through the front door
with two monster firemen
doublehanding coal with steel shovels
and grunting like angry rhinos

Peek out the window. Chagrin.
See a fat bull elk rubbing the velvet
off his antlers on my doorjamb

Enraged, I leap outside reckless
and hurled a bucket at his head
which missed, and landed among
the grazing horses which stampeded
from the naked madman,

who now sits on his porch
pink skinned, having given up on sleep
to stare at the world revealed by a silver moon.

Silent Ken
Paul St. Pierre

Big Creek — When I suggested to Kenny Skomoroh that we take a couple of horses and try to pick up a moose, it was below freezing and the wind was driving snow horizontal to the ground.

"Okay," he said.

I discussed the weather and the behavior of moose at such times. Would they be in the timber or in the meadows? Would they be spooky? In short, were we likely to get a shot, all things considered?

"Maybe," he said.

We left the ranch at first light in a Merc one-ton truck that should have gone long ago to the Great Car Lot in The Sky. Half an hour later we got stuck.

"Damn," said Kenny.

He worked us loose. We went on and stuck again.

"Hell," he said.

The third time we stuck he didn't offer any comments.

He spun the wheels. He shovelled. He spun some more. He unslung the chains, got out the jack, fixed the jack, jacked the jack, bruised his hands, haywired the chains, plied the pliers, and used a screw-driver for a chisel, with slush down his neck and mud on his face and the truck and two horses threatening to topple on him from the rickety jack and end it all.

Like other men of the country, he has the skill, the patience and the endurance to take that old truck up a mountain and load it with glacier ice or fly it to the sky and snatch golden apples from the sun, once his mind is made up to it.

He got the chains on and raced the motor.

One chain came loose and whistled away over a meadow.

"Bastard," said Kenny.

He was up to two syllables.

He took off the chain and rocked the truck out, drove two more miles, backed the truck against a snowdrift to unload the horses off the tailgate and it stuck again.

I asked him if this meant we would have to try chaining up again when we rode back here in the dark.

"Probably," he said.

Then I asked him which horse was mine.

"The brown," he said.

That shows once again that most people talk more than is necessary.

If I'd waited until he got aboard his pinto, it would have been made quite clear to me that I was riding the brown and there wouldn't have been all that talk.

PARTNERS

(above) Often a cowboy had only his bedroll and a saddle. If he found a ranch that had a good horse for him to ride he would stay, if not he would drift on to another place and another, until he found a horse that worked easily with him and became his partner.

RIDING TALL

(right) It took a long time to paint this big bearskin coat. I liked the pattern that the fur formed. The coat was the kind worn by a ranger, almost ground length to keep his legs warm and split high up the back so it fell on either side of the saddle. There's a sense of silence deep in the darkness of the forest.

L.GIBBS

After that I left conversation to Kenny.

Four hours later he talked some more. He stopped his horse, got off, tied it, and started building a fire.

"Dinner time," he said.

Later that day he pointed at a few poles on the edge of a meadow.

"Camped there once."

I pointed to a squared poplar post. "There's something written there," I said.

"Franklin," he said.

If I knew who or what Franklin was, he needn't say more. If I needed to know more, I could ask. The system works very well.

I did not ask.

Late in the afternoon I said I reckoned we had cut the tracks of three moose.

"I'd say four," he said.

We didn't keep that argument going any longer.

Sometimes we walked to get warm. On the horses we sat, feet frozen in the stirrups, hunched over, looking at the saddle horn as if there was an important message written on it.

He spoke five times to his horse. Three times he said, "Huhu, huhu." The other times he called it a knothead and a son of a bitch.

When the day was old and the sky was coloring, he stopped his pinto and held up one hand. Then pointed to a moose in the jackpines. Only bulls are legal.

"Cow," he said.

There wasn't anything more to say on that subject, so we rode back to the truck, fought mud, snow, chains and sulky cayuses and got back to the ranch deep in the darkness. They asked what kind of a day we had had.

"Cold," said Kenny.

Angling
Colin Fletcher

An addiction to fishing can do many things for a man, but none of them quite compares with the way it can, very occasionally, defeat the clock.

A boy of six or eight or thirteen starts every new day expecting a miracle or two to happen before sunset. Put a fishing rod in his hand, and expectation edges toward certainty. In bright morning sunlight he hurries down the familiar trail that leads to the river. As he goes, he saves precious fishing time by gulping down his sandwich lunch. He reaches the river — and the whole, wide, exciting world narrows down to that first, still-uncaught fish.

In due time the boy becomes a man. He may, unfortunately, atrophy into a grim-faced fish slayer. But if he grows up he finds that the catching of fish comes to matter less and less. He savors subtler joys — joys that he refuses to examine too closely for fear analysis will shatter them. But he knows, though he rarely admits it even to himself, that somehow, somewhere along the line, he has lost something.

The years pass. Then chance provides the right company or the right solitude, the right elation or the right despair, the right sunlight or the right rain. And to

these is added, at the right time and place, some new and piquant element. It trips a tumbler. Something the man has almost forgotten wells up inside him; for a brief interlude he recaptures his youth.

Such interludes are very rare. But the man remembers them for the rest of his life.

During the month of hectic planning back in San Francisco, I had spoken on the phone one day to a friend named Herb Pintler in the California Fish and Game Department.

"Guess you'll be going through Alpine Country," he said. "I know a place up there just made for you. Wild country it is. Almost untouched. A little creek called Silver King with special cutthroat trout that not many people know about. Isolated variants they are, quite different from ordinary cutthroats. Beautiful little fish. Would you like some literature on them?"

"Surely," I said. "I doubt if I'll be able to spend any time there but . . . ."

Herb had laughed quietly into the phone. "Once you get up there," he said, "you'll make time."

Even then, before I knew any more, I think I felt something stir inside me. And, when, high above the West

Walker River, I climbed the final snowbank into a ten-thousand foot pass, I knew at last what I had heard in Herb Pintler's voice. Beyond the snowbank, the mountainside dropped away again. And there below me lay the valley of the Silver King.

Timbered slopes plunged down a twisting V that held the creek. Two miles downstream a meadow showed emerald green. Beyond, peak after Sierra peak stretched away northward to the horizon. There was no sign that a man's hand had touched a single leaf or blade of grass.

As I dug my staff in the snow to ease the weight of the pack, I knew for certain what I had suspected all along: that I was going to find much more in the Silver King than a special kind of trout. Already I could feel the valley's fascination. Deep shadow covered its far slopes. From the shadow, treetops thrust up like green stalagmites into slanting sunshine. The contrast and interplay between sunlight and shadow gave the place a leprechaun air of almost-too-perfect enchantment.

After a while I began to walk down the mountainside. The snow ended. Trees began again. Among the pines and firs giant junipers appeared, the spiraling bark of their orange trunks reaching up sixty feet and more. A doe stared at me from the far side of the clearing, uncertain whether to be frightened. A bar of sunlight, piercing the forest shadow, floodlit a crimson columbine. Then I reached the first shrill water of the creek and walked through beds of sunflowers and lupines and scarlet Indian paintbrush.

By the time I pitched camp, the creek had matured. Its pools had taken on that depth — a certain depth of color rather than any linear measure — that every trout fisherman knows means fish. But somehow the urge to fish did not come. I did not mind though. I knew the fish

would wait. For I knew that this beautiful little valley had been kept hidden away in secrecy for no one but me. And the knowledge was no less exciting because the grown-up, down-to-earth part of me knew that it was complete nonsense.

WILLOW CREEK

(previous page) The aging dog in this painting belonged to an adult couple. Usually she didn't have any children to play with, but when these two turned up for a visit, she had a marvellous day with them. She seemed to sense that they were young and even when they were all having fun together she kept a rather protective eye on them.

The Mustang Colt
Robert Kroetsch

The first time Hazard saw the mustang colt that was to be founder of the line — the first time he saw *them*, I should say, for there were two of them, the mustang and the Cree — they were together in the middle of Wildfire Lake.

It was as if they had just bobbed to the surface. Hazard had looked a minute earlier and there was nothing to be seen but whitecaps. He was up on a high bank that is almost a cliff; he was there partly just to look, partly because he was homesick for the sight of a little water. The flat parklands break suddenly, and you see a valley — not in front of you, below you. The squares of farmland are gone and below you a wooded coulee, like the crack in a fat lady's ass, guides a scar of earth down to a long narrow lake. The man in the water wasn't riding the horse; he was swimming beside it with his arm around its neck, as if one or the other of them was about to drown.

Hazard raced down the hill so recklessly he might have broken every bone in his body. He stripped off his green plaid mackinaw — it was a raw windy day in late fall. He was a harvester then, come west for the first time, and he was unbearably homesick. He kicked off his boots and started into that cold lake; but just as he did so

the swimmer, who as I say turned out to be a Cree — at least I discovered years later there were some Crees at the outlet of the lake that fall, drying fish — got into the shallows and managed to stand up. He was pulling not a horse but a very young colt, his arm around its neck. The colt was so exhausted it had quit trying, and the Indian was pulling it through the water.

Just as Hazard got his crotch wet, however, the Indian stepped into a hole. Then Hazard too hit deep water and had to strike out swimming, but Hazard practically grew up in water. The Indian came to the surface and went down again; indeed he had gone down for the third time, still clinging to the colt, when Hazard dived, and in the green haze of that pure water caught hold of the man's black hair and hauled him up headfirst.

A strange thing happened. Hazard should have told the man to let go of the colt so they'd stand a decent chance of getting to shore. Instead he pitched in like a madman, thrashing and struggling to save both.

When they got onto the sandbar, the Cree knelt to massage the colt's heart, gasping for breath himself, unable to get to his own feet. Hazard began to feel very much the intruder; he walked ashore and busied himself putting on his boots — only to turn on an impulse and

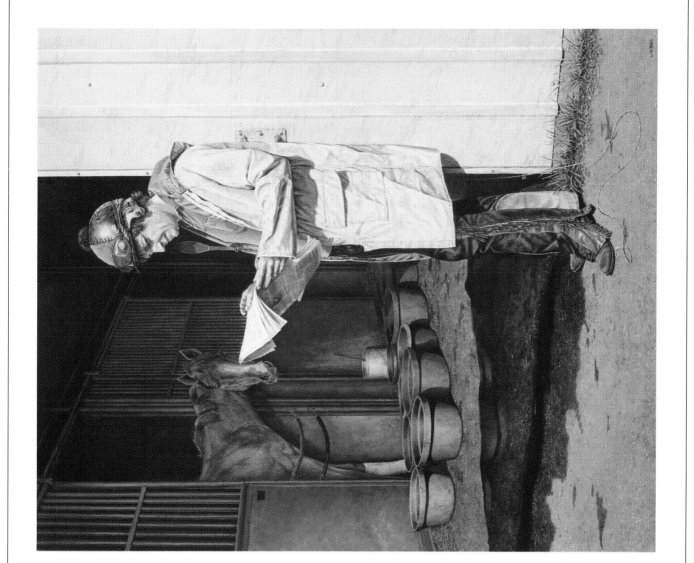

WASHING DOWN

(left) Rather than paint jockeys in their colorful silks, I did a series of paintings backstage at the racetrack. This was done very early in the morning, with the steam rising off the horse which has just come in from being exercised.

I got to know a lot about these long-legged, skittish animals and I liked the way this one kept a close eye on me at all times.

CHECKING THE FORM

(right) The trainer, one of the most important men at the track, is responsible for the care, grooming, exercise and diet of one or several horses. Each horse has a different feed formula and you can see the feed mixing tubs in the background, one for each horse in the stable. The horses that will be racing that day don't get fed until after the race and while their stable mates are happily munching they make it pretty obvious that they're feeling neglected.

walk, boots and all, back into the water. He carried the Indian, then the colt, out onto the beach. It was a male colt, a stallion. Hazard studied first the colt, then the Indian, and noticed the latter had in his long hair a couple of very fat lice; they too had narrowly escaped from drowning. I saved them too, he thought to himself and chuckled even while he panted. He shivered from the raw wind on his wet clothes; he stood shivering, chuckling, panting like an utter idiot, yet he was unable to tear himself away.

The colt opened his big gentle eyes and the Cree turned to Hazard for the first time, grinning now. Hazard was startled, for the Indian had the physique of a young man; yet his few remaining teeth looked nothing less than ancient.

"I saved your colt," the Indian said.

"It isn't mine."

The Indian smiled his disbelief. "Don't fear. I shall demand nothing."

Hazard started to answer, but instead he picked up his mackinaw and knelt and began rubbing fiercely at the colt's pale blue silky coat. He paused to wring the icy water from his beard, then would not waste time on anything so trivial.

Now, while Hazard labored, the Indian stood watching.

"I demand nothing," he repeated.

He was wearing only moccasins and a pair of badly soiled tweed dress trousers. He pulled something that looked like an eagle feather from his pocket and stuck it into one of his braids. Then — and Hazard swore to this — he brought out a small pocket mirror and looked at himself. "I saved your colt," he said.

"It's not mine," Hazard tried to explain. "I'm a

stranger here myself."

The Indian's old teeth were beginning to chatter; he had been in the water a long time. He said something like, *Kis-see-wus-kut-ta-o*. "Stranger," Hazard said. He guessed that perhaps the Indian spoke little English. "Me stranger. Me no live here."

The Indian shook his head. His teeth were chattering uncontrollably. "I do not wish to be thanked. It is enough to have saved your colt." *Kis-see-wus-kut-ta-o.*

"Wait a minute," Hazard said. "Hang on." The Cree gave the impression that he was about to leave. "You can't just take off. You can't just march away from this motherless colt. My God, it'll die of starvation. You can't just stick a feather into your bonnet and go hightailing off into the weeds. We'll have to find out who owns —"

But indeed the Indian had gone.

The Horsemen

THE ALBERTAN

This man was such a classic example of ranchers everywhere that I asked him to pose for me, and he did while he was waiting for another group of animals to be brought in for branding. It's tough work and his quarter horse was content to wait patiently, too. Ranchers gather from miles around to help each other during this busy season and their wives gather in the kitchen to prepare mountains of food.

WAITING FOR THE HERD

Painted just because I liked the composition. I took particular pleasure in his sun-bleached jacket, the jeans he'd snagged on barbed wire, and the finger poking out of the worn leather gloves. Everything looks hot and dusty, but storm clouds are rolling in.

A Cattleman's Story
Hugh Lynch-Staunton

You can always tell a cattleman. He's the fellow whose face looks as though it's worn out three bodies.

It's a job that keeps you working seven days a week — cattle don't know it's Sunday.

There were small herds of cattle in this south west corner of Alberta from the days of the first settlers but it was really in 1876 that the industry got its start. The story goes that a bull and fourteen cows were driven up to Fort Macleod from Montana and that a sergeant in the Northwest Mounted Police won them in a poker game. Without time, money or hay the sergeant was forced to turn them loose on the range for the winter. To everyone's surprise they survived and each cow had a calf. People realized that cattle could survive without feed, although many would find that outside the Chinook belt this policy could lead to disaster. Even here, in a bad winter, some ranchers lost half of their herds and my grandfather tells of seeing carcasses that had frozen to death standing. Many ranchers were forced to sell out and the remaining ones realized the necessity of having winter feed available.

When my grandfather was married he and his new bride drove to Lethbridge in a buggy for a honeymoon. He bought an old house and moved it to the ranch with twenty-four horses. He said that the only way this was possible was because all of the horses couldn't make up their minds to run away at the same time. My dad lives in that house today.

In conjunction with his cattle operations my grandfather and his brother ran butcher shops in Pincher Creek, Blairmore, Fernie and Cranbrook. These were profitable businesses until their accountant took off with a suitcase full of money. This forced the sale of the meat markets, dissolved grandfather's ranching partnership and placed the family in debt for many years. In those days books were kept by the bank. You wrote cheques until the bank told you you were out of money. Then you borrowed from the bank. When you sold cattle you turned the money over to the bank.

We're all familiar with stories of the depression. The climate was bad and prices were low. The start of the war in 1939 marked the end of the depression but posed an additional strain on the livestock industry. Shortages and lack of manpower slowed the recovery. Cattlemen voluntarily stopped cattle exports to the United States in order to sell to Britain. Their income suffered. My dad was away training soldiers and my grandfather and an elderly hired man kept the place together.

Victory marked the beginning of prosperity for the cattleman and prices strengthened. Truck movement of cattle became commonplace. This meant more accessibility to the market place and also a spread of livestock diseases. In 1952 foot and mouth disease

slammed the U.S. border shut leaving Canada with a cattle surplus. Prices fell and didn't recover to that level again for twenty years.

Veterinarians became more numerous in the fifties. They worked like hell and got poorly paid but along the way they educated a lot of us and brought the technology of animal health to the country.

In the sixties the dam of technology burst — meat science, genetics, forages, fertilizers, silages, feed conversions and other innovations were begun. I wasn't paying attention. I had just sold two cows to buy a three hundred dollar engagement ring.

In 1966 the Simmental bull "Parisien" arrived and pushed the cattle industry into the "exotic boom." This is over now but it was the "gold rush," of the cattle business. It filled us with hope and optimism, forced technologies on us, and most important, blew away the lethargy that had crept into our thinking. We hear of fortunes lost but there were also mortgages paid off, new houses built and improvements and modernization done during this time.

We've seen a host of diseases run rampant and brought under control. We've used A.I., R.O.P., crossbreeding and embryo transplants. We've used Canfax, become familiar with cow cycles, volatile prices and have imported breeding cattle from the U.S., England and Germany.

In 1976 our ranch became debt free for the first time in three generations. Two years later we were back in.

A cattleman? He's proud, independent and resourceful. His tenacity keeps him working harder for less. He cherishes his freedom and through all the booms and busts, he doesn't quit.

RANGER

(left) The orange and black scarf is another item that often comes out of my "costume" box. It adds a striking flash of color to an otherwise somber painting.

HIGH COUNTRY RANGER

(above) In high country, rangers check, count and evaluate the herds of mountain sheep and mountain goats to make sure that they are in good condition and that there is nothing developing that needs to be corrected. I put a corner of light in the painting to give an indication of elevation.

Shawn
Sid Marty

There is a strange sensation in the point of balance when a saddle starts to fall off, and the body lists slowly to the right in a kind of impromptu Immelman turn. Strange because the numbed synapses in my butt and knees were temporarily out of service, so my brain was short on stimulus-response type information.

The eyes telegraphed what they were seeing; "Aiee! Ground getting close."

And the brain replied: "Am taking evasive action." But it came too late. I found myself sliding crazily under the gelding's belly to land with a crash on the ground.

The old stud hopped sideways and pulled at the end of his lines which were still clutched in my left hand. The saddle and blankets had slid halfway down his ribs. Since I had dropped the halter rope, I looked anxiously for the mare who stood patiently biting the grass beside the trail, eyes politely averted from the humiliating spectacle.

Shawn, I learned later had been "holding out on me," a favorite trick of greedy junkies and cinch-wise horses. He'd sucked himself full of hot air back in the corral when I cinched him up and then he'd let it out later. There were two good inches of slack between the woven cinch band and the gelding's breast bone.

I tidied it all up and tightened the cinch again, ignoring the gelding's protestations that it was too tight. He was one of those phony plugs that moaned and

groaned as soon as you touched the latigo, hoping he could con you into leaving it loose. Since then, I've seen a few old cowboys let the wind out of this kind of scam with a sudden boot in the guts. I was lucky not to know that trick because when it came to kicking, Shawn definitely had me outclassed.

With the cinch tight, I stepped on and started to swing my right leg up. But I had committed the sin of the slack rein, which is otherwise known as the Big Step, the Lift-off, or the Cemetery Leap. With the left rein slack, the gelding was able to bog his head, that is, get it down low enough to obtain the leverage he needed to really sock it to me. One fast buck was enough to make sure I never found my seat. It helped to magnify the slight arc begun when I threw the right leg up. He put a little top on me, I was airborne without a parachute.

A big dome-shaped boulder came up like a howdydoo and I landed on it, chest first. The wind went out of me and I remember thinking that it wasn't coming back in this world. The lights blinked on and off and shuffled into a wild kaleidoscope. The pain was severe.

How long I lay there, coiled into a foetal ball, I don't know. But the cold shadows of the spruce were stretching across me and the sun was half way down the big wall of the Vice-President before I even dreamed of getting up.

79

Earlier, I had seen a bear sign on the trail, so the cold lick of a long wet tongue on my neck almost finished the pain with a terminal heart attack. I eased slowly around after a minute and came eye to eyeball with the mare, towering above me. Her ears lifted with mild interest to see that I wasn't yet a corpse.

It doesn't do to get hurt alone in the mountains, several miles from the nearest radio or road. The temperature at night can drop to near freezing, and without extra clothing or a fire, an injured man could lapse into hypothermia. I thought that they'd find me in a day or two with clothes ripped off in my delerium and a nasty grimace on my face. Perhaps I would leave them a little note telling them where they could shove their horses.

These unpleasant thoughts, coupled with the fading warmth of the sun, inspired me to try my bruised limbs. There was a tender area on my chest which was swelling into a lemon sized lump, but all the hinges worked, and there didn't seem to be any spokes poking inconveniently into any lungs.

My reluctant charger pawed impatiently at the ground. His reins had tangled in a deadfall and stopped him from galloping home in riderless triumph. The red haze in front of my eyes made it difficult to focus on the gelding, as I hauled myself carefully toward him by the branches of a handy spruce. Sensing my frame of mind, he danced warily backwards into the shadows, teeth and eyeballs flashing. I lunged forward and grabbed the lines. Shawn went up over me, striking the air with his forefeet. No longer caring, I laughed a malicious chuckle.

"Gotcha, you slippery sonofabitch," I cried. "Now I'm gonna give you your lumps."

Crazed notion. Hundred-and-eighty-pound greenhorn versus 1,000 pound hammerhead. I punched wildly as he came down, hitting him a glancing blow on his rock-hard jaw that nearly broke my wrist. The shooting pain that went up my arm would have popped my skull off had I not already flipped my lid. Shawn snorted and tap-danced on the rocky trail, while I hopped and hollered my frustrated pain and rage. It was the fear that I suddenly noticed in the mare's eye that snapped me out of it. If I was reduced to sparring with my horse this early in the game, I might as well pack the whole job in tomorrow.

Full of real despair, I sat down and calmed my nerves with a bowl of tobacco and thought it over. It was pretty obvious that up until now the gelding had mastered me and, if I wanted the job, I would have to master him, starting immediately. I couldn't outmuscle him so I'd have to outsmart him. Somehow.

Shawn and I had a little talk about far pastures and dog food factories while I lengthened the stirrups, and with threats dire, hauled myself painfully into the saddle. His only response was to roll his sensuous old lip over his yellow teeth, breaking into a trot for home, and nearly unsaddling me again as Bess took up the slack. Not that I needed the halter. Both nags could smell hay at least four miles upwind. As long as the direction was home, they needed no prompting from me.

In the months that followed, Shawn was absolutely merciless. Whenever I stepped behind him, he would show me the white of his eye, depress his ears, and cock one back foot for a kick that never quite came. I guess he aimed to wear me out with suspense. But he taught me a lot. He taught me never to take anything for granted, to keep my eyes peeled for trouble, speaking softly and moving slowly. He taught me how to survive.

THE ORPHAN

Every ranch kid shares the chores according to his age and ability. The job for this little boy, the youngest in the family, was to feed this ravenous young calf several times a day.

The Horseman
Jim Gibson

My mother's family were Alberta ranchers. Her grandfather was an early manager of one of the first ranching companies. His family was Virginia gentry, and, reputedly, he was its black sheep — at least, the only one we knew about. He ended up in the Canadian west trailing a herd of cattle from Montana.

My great grandfather was said to be a difficult man. It was even rumored he had notches in his gun; a source of great fascination to me, a kid growing up in Toronto in the days of television cowboys.

Much as I would have liked to boast that my great-grandad ended up as a notch in someone else's gun, he didn't. However, he died the next best way as far as a pistol packin' Toronto kid was concerned; he was thrown from a horse in the Calgary Stampede. The story lost a little in later years when I learned it wasn't a bucking bronc that finished him off, but a saddle horse he rode in a parade of old-timers.

My father's family was from Northern Ontario. They were contractors and prospectors. But, as a youngster, "the north," never had the same allure for me as "the west." It had to do with horses.

My father's boyhood stories were of buildings and machinery, stories that might be expected of a man who became an engineer. Most often, my mother's stories centered on horses and, indirectly, the lessons she had learned from them.

She made horses sound like teachers from the most practical of schools — the sort who'd willingly give any fool enough rope and then laugh when he hung himself. But if your mistakes were innocent enough, she said, they were forgiving. The point was to be honest and up front. Never be blunderingly bold nor, worse, fearful. Otherwise they'd get you every time.

My childhood catechism was more than the expected, "Look both ways before you cross the street." It included other irrefutable truths: Speak before approaching a colt from behind; Never ride alone in the hills; walk the first mile out and the last mile home.

It was a long time before I had a chance to put those truths into practice. Of course, there were still horses in the streets of Toronto. However, our meetings were not the sort to cause great-grandfather to rein up on his Pegasus and beam down with pride.

There was the time I wondered what would happen if I slapped the side of the milkwagon the way the milkman did. Would the horse trot off down the street without him? It did.

By the time I reached school age we had moved to the suburbs and I fostered dreams of a pony for the back yard. I eventually gave up on it, settling instead for bike rides to nearby riding stables or any field where I knew there to be a horse.

The most significant book for me wasn't the expected *My Friend Flicka* or *The Black Stallion*. Instead, it was my mother's photograph album. I wasn't particularly interested in the pages documenting her days at an Okanagan girls' school, family trips to Banff, and the first time my father took her home to Northern Ontario. Rather, it was the earlier pages, the ones with pictures of her family and their horses. Even now, I can rhyme off the names of my favorites — Pixie, Actress, Glen Bow and the stallion from England, Vambrace — printed in white ink below.

I remember one photo of my grandfather lined up with his brothers on a Calgary polo field. There was another of him taking the saddle horses over to winter in the hills. That picture always bothered me. There seemed something ominous and cruel about it. However, my mother always insisted that horses that wintered free in the hills always returned fatter in the spring than those who stuck close to the barn. It was another of those all-encompassing truths I've yet to shake.

Much of my mother's album made her corner of the Canadian west look like something Mazo de la Roche would have used for inspiration if she'd set her Jalna books in Alberta. It was polo, lawn tennis and newly-constructed kennels for my grandmother's dogs from England. There weren't a lot of cowboys in the album for a youngster nurtured in the old west by American television.

One exception was my mother's oldest brother. He was always photographed in a stock saddle. He was later killed in Italy and it was him that I focused on during school Remembrance Day services. I'd conjure up those photographs, showing him as a handsome kid in a floppy big hat and chaps, grinning out at the camera from a downright homely horse. That horse wasn't flashy, but I knew he would never have let my uncle down.

I was twelve before I ever made it to the west. I arrived with the most romantic preconceptions — all of them concerning horses. I knew that once a cowboy dropped his reins on the ground his horse would stay beside him. My own test of that was later to put me on the ground with two broken arms.

I also knew that all western horses had an innate ability to chase, corner and otherwise corral cows. On my first visit, my uncle had me mounted on Ed, a buckskin of at least twice my years. My cousins and I had brought some cattle up to the corrals where my uncle was working the gates. One old cow ducked out, passed my uncle and headed straight for Ed. I grabbed the horn, loosened the reins and waited for old Ed to do his stuff. The cow scooted passed Ed's nose and headed off to freedom.

My uncle swore at me. I choked back tears, never quite explaining that I thought Ed was supposed to do it all on his own.

Where The Sun Sets

THE BEACHCOMBERS

(left) Whenever you walk along the shore the ever present gulls flock down, watching curiously and hoping for a handout. Kids find treasures on the beach too: pretty shells, feathers, sand polished wood and wild flowers.

ROUNDING THE WINDWARD MARKER

(above) I was an honorary crew member of Canada 1 when the team trained off the west coast. The fast action and thrill of the race were something I hoped to capture here. This particular sail configuration, with the mainsail, foresail and spinakker all in use, is of only a few seconds duration. I had the crew chief double check this painting for accuracy.

Sea Anchor
Kevin Roberts

The wind and sea grew and the main line and the deep line on the starboard side crossed and tangled and for half an hour he struggled to bring both of them in and clear the gear. The skipper watched, red-eyed, and finally told him to pull all the lines in and lash them down.

Incredibly, though the skipper stopped regularly to retch overboard, Mel worked with him until all the gear was on board and the lines and lead cannonballs lashed down with cutty hunk. Together they pulled the prostrate Bert into the wheelhouse and down into the bunk. Bill went out again to the stern, staggered back with armful after armful of salmon, crawled deep down into the hold of the boat, stuffed handfuls of ice into the cleaned bellies of the fish and stacked them into the waiting ice.

"Sea-anchor, Bill," mumbled Mel pointing to the bow. "I'll run the boat up, you drop it." Bill looked through the window. The weighted parachute with the red Scotsman buoy was lashed to the foredeck. It had to be eased overboard so it sank and opened deep beneath the sea. A long rope, coiled now on the bow, then ran from the capstan on the bow down to the chute flowering under the sea. With this down the boat rode easily, moving with the tide a mile or so in and out, on the ballooned tension of the underwater anchor. But it was dangerous to put out

in a high wind. If the chute snapped open in the gale the rope would whip out like a snake striking. If the boat was not held tight against the smashing swell, the rope jerked about and the feet and body of the man, already threatened by the great wash of water pounding against it, could be washed overboard, instantly. The very idea of walking out there, out to where the grey sea bounded onto the bow, was almost too much for him, except for the haggard look of the skipper, white faced and red eyed. He knew then that he had to do it, not just for them on the boat, but for himself, because the sea was building relentlessly and it was doubtful if they could turn and run safely back before it. The danger of broaching, or of the stern going under in the massive rolling seas was such that he looked an instant at Mel, and saw in his watering eyes that there was only one choice.

And he had shuffled grimly out along the deck, gripping the handrail tightly with both hands, past the wheelhouse and out onto the bow. There, the first burst of swell knocked him soaking and breathless to his knees. Worse, the suck of the sea off the deck rushed about him and loosened his footing. In the second or two before the next wave burst upon him, he worked with one hand on the lashed parachute. He timed his work so that in the

brief dip of the bow, before the next swell deluged him, the parachute and its chain and rope were freed. He hooked one foot about a stanchion, braced the other, and in the same two-second dip, let the parachute and rope slip through his left hand over the side. Despite his efforts the rope kicked and jumped and burnt his wrist and hand.

It was not classic seamanship. There were many men of the West Coast fishing fleet for whom this act was daily bread, but for him, the final "tung" of the rope, tight against the capstan, the red Scotsman floating before the boat now easing back, was a gong of triumph. He sat, hanging on to the rail, his knees braced against the stanchion, totally exhausted, wet through and not at all jubilant. His hands were scored and torn by the rope. He thought of the poached salmon steaks he'd seen once for an exorbitant price, served in silver chafers in a restaurant on Sloane Square in London and the enormity of the callous economics of it made him burst out with laughter. Eventually he crawled back on his knees, gripping the rail, and got into the wheelhouse.

SUN HAT

The painting is round to echo the shape of the sun and the concentric circles of the sun hat. I balanced for hours on top of a ladder in soft sand to get this painting and kept almost falling off, much to the amusement of the model.

BIRDS

I saw a girl wearing a light cape on the beach one day and the swirling fabric reminded me of flight. The model posed for me, looking out to the horizon and beyond. I used the flight pattern of the gulls to reinforce the feeling of freedom.

The Island
David Conover

The island was a great teacher. There is a keen sense of joy in acquiring new skills and disciplines, in learning the rhythm of the tide without consulting the little grey book, in understanding the whims of weather and sea. Heavy dew meant a clear day ahead, and dark, low scurrying clouds meant an angry sea. Every day we learned something new — often without knowing it, and most often about ourselves. Man is a marvel of adaptability. Little comes along that he either cannot bear or change to suit himself. We learned, too, that in every step there must be a compromise — between what we wanted to do and what we could do within our means and strength. Unlike the city, where we waited for each day to end, longing for the four o'clock whistle, now the days never seemed long enough. Our hearts ached as twilight brought them to a close.

Before, we had been only half alive. Now, lean from hard work and bronzed by the sun, we felt wonderfully limber and strong. Three months had done wonders for us physically. We had spring to our steps, a feeling of well-being. We had calluses crossed our palms instead of blisters. That mark of frantic living, the look of tenseness on Jeanne's face, had changed to a deep serenity — she was more beautiful than ever.

Our senses, dulled by civilization, were springing to life. We could tell, by their scent, a dozen different wildflowers and spot a widow-maker high in the arms of a mighty fir that at first had been only a green blur. The simple food had sharpened our taste. It began with Jeanne's homemade bread, which tasted even better than it smelled — not like the flavorless fluff we bought at home. Vegetables, picked, cooked and eaten the same hour taste like nothing from a freezer or can.

But to top everything, we had a new conception of an egg. Our eggs bore little resemblance to their city cousins. Two beliefs had been shattered: the holiness of a white egg and the food value of a sickly yellow yolk. The color of the shell, we found, had no bearing on the contents — it was correlated with the color of the feathers. But the most astonishing difference was in the yolks. Ours were dark orange and loaded with vitamins from hens that ate natural greens outside the run. Under the old fashioned grading system, brown shells and dark yolks were both frowned on — a loss of the farmer's pocket and the consumer's health. An egg that comes from an unfettered hen, which you own body and soul, tastes like none you'll ever cart home from a supermarket. The city had made us immune to sound. At first, the stillness of the forest frightened us. The Island's silence made us nervous and apprehensive, conscious that we were a frail bit of matter in an unfriendly environment. The slightest noise startled us.

Slowly, as the weeks slipped by, the silence we thought so great disappeared. The island breathed with constant sound, the rustlings and twitterings in the bush, the drone of bees and insects, and the ceaseless murmur of the sea. We no longer needed the comforting blare of the radio. Life had bestowed upon us an unexpected gift. Our untrained ears had found the magical wavelength that made up our world. From a distance we could easily identify the marauding seal by its sudden burst to the surface, gasping for air; the weird fluted cry of the loon and the playful barks of the sea otter frolicking in the cove.

SPLICING LINE

(above) The life of a working sailor is constantly involved with repair as water, wind and waves take their toll on his boat. A sailor makes do with the tools at hand and though splicing line should be done with a marlin spike, this man uses a sharp steel wedge. I felt the "make do" situation was in keeping with the rusty Polish fish packer in the background.

CALL OF THE SEA

(right) Pulled up on the rocks and abandoned, this old wooden boat has seen years of service . . . an ideal place for a boy to climb aboard and dream of the sailing adventures he will have some day. The birds convey a feeling of freedom and escape.

Blue Highways
William Least Heat Moon

U.S. 20; a scribble of a road, a line drawn by a palsied engineer. The route was small farms — one with a covered bridge — and small pastures and mountainsides of maple and fir and alder and wet green moss. Oblique sunlight turned blossoms of Scotch broom into yellow incandescence that illumined the highway; settlers brought the plant from Scotland to use in broommaking, but it had escaped cultivation and is now a nuisance to coastal farmers as well as a fine ornament of spring.

The road squeezed through a narrow pass, then dropped to Yaquina Bay with its long arches of bridging. In the distance, the blue Pacific shot silver all the way to the horizon. I had come to the other end of the continent.

Newport has been a tourist town for more than a century and it showed: a four lane runway of beef-and-bun joints and seashell shops; city blocks where beach bungalows jammed in salty shingle to shiplap. On north to Agate Beach. Shoreline I had camped on fifteen years before was now glassy condominiums and the path to the ocean posted. Again northward to a pocket of shore between developments near Cape Foulweather. The surf rolled out an unbroken roar like a waterfall rather than the intermittent crash I'd listened to in North Carolina. In the

lee of a big tussock of beach grass I ate lunch, as gulls, slipping over the drafts and yawing and tilting in the stiff sea wind, watched me watch them. It's a curious sensation when nature looks back.

I stayed so long that dark clouds moved in and piled against the mountains like flotsam washed ashore. Then it began to hail. Cape Foulweather, named by Captain James Cook exactly two hundred years earlier, showed itself true, and I cursed and ran for the truck. By the time I reached Depoe Bay a few miles up the coast, the western sky had cleared again, and the afternoon sun seemed to glare off the ocean all the way from the orient. Cycles. The cold waves, coming unimpeded from Japan six thousand miles away, struck the rocks hard, and the high surf so struggled, it looked as though the sea were trying either to get out or pull the shore back in.

A high concrete-arch bridge crossed a narrow zigzag cleft of an inlet leading to a small harbor under the cliffs. Depoe Bay used to be a picturesque fishing village; now it was just picturesque. The fish houses, but for one seasonal company, were gone, the fleet gone, and in their stead had come sport fishing boats and souvenir ashtray and T-shirt shops. In Depoe Bay the big fish now was the tourist, and, like grunion, its run was seasonal swarming.

Several streets scotched the town but you could forget them all except the big one: U.S. 101. What happened economically happened on 101 or the water. Two restaurants faced the highway: one called the Happy Harpooner or some silliness; the other had no sign visible. A beanery needing no name had to be good. As if suspended above the harbor, it sat on a cliff with all comings and goings of men and boats and tide and wind in complete view.

I took a plate of fresh bottomfish, chowder and slaw. At the next table four charterboat seamen, watch caps pulled tightly to their skulls, bent into the vapor of coffee mugs, and talked about snapped shafts, leaking holding tanks, environmental regulations, creosoted timbers. Down in the harbor, cabin lights blinked on and bobbed in the dusk. I asked a seaman who sat alone if I could park overnight on the waterfront. "Coast Guard station down there surveys things close," he said. "Why don't you take a state campground?"

"I'd rather see Oregon than trailers from Ohio."

The man operated a charterboat company that catered to tourists. He said this: "Depoe Bay used to be a good commercial fishing town, but they overfished this corner of the Pacific. Then they polluted the spawning streams. Maybe the big schools will come back, maybe not. I don't care. My sport boats are easier and income's more predictable — can't always land greenling, but you can always hook a Californian. But there was a time when all those wood buildings on the bay processed our catch, back when the commission gave out commercial fishing licenses to anybody. Then we started getting irresponsible jackboats ruining the grounds. Next year, to get a license, you'll have to earn sixty per cent of your income from fishing. Going to keep out the exploiters."

"Changes everywhere."

"This coast is a story of one thing after another disappearing. Except people. We don't have sea otters much now, but you used to see them floating on their backs with a flat rock on their stomachs, cracking open shellfish on it. Razor clams hard as hell to find now. Beach used to have agates, petrified wood, Japanese net floats — those colored glass balls you know. Pieces of broken up schooners, too. Coast was full of skookums. That's what the Chinooks called ghosts. Know what you'll find beachcombing now? Clorox jugs."

LIFTING FOG

(overleaf) In this age of high tech plastic boats and gasoline engines, I always enjoy seeing an old wooden dinghy being rowed. The model here is a true sailor who has sailed the oceans of the world. We had the boat tied to the dock so he wouldn't row off into the sunset while I painted him.

Becker
Jack Hodgins

Becker, the first time you see him, is at the mainland terminus waving your car down the ramp onto the government ferry and singing to your headlights and to the salt air and to the long line of traffic behind you that he'd rather be a sparrow than a snail. Yes, he would if he could, he loudly sings, he surely would. In his orange life jacket and fluorescent gloves, he waves his arms to direct traffic down that ramp the way someone else might conduct a great important orchestra — a round little man with a sloppy wool cap riding his head and a huge bushy beard hiding all of his face except the long turned-down weather-reddened nose. He'd rather be a forest, he sings than a street.

Follow him home.

Ride the ferry with him on its two-hour trip across the Strait of Georgia, while the long backbone ridge of the island's mountains sharpens into blue and ragged shades of green, and the coastline shadows shape themselves into rock cliffs and driftwood-cluttered bays; then follow him up the ramp, the end of his shift, as he sets out through the waiting lines of traffic and gusts of rushing passengers on foot. No longer the serenading conductor, he is a short stump of a man walking down the full length of the waterfront parking lot and then up the

long slow hill towards the town, his black overcoat hanging down past the tops of his rubber boots suggesting the shape of a squat crockery jug. He stops to explore the rain water running through the limp grass in the ditch, and to talk for a while with someone leaning over a front-porch ledge, to buy a pocketful of candy in a corner store. But eventually he gets into his old fenderless green Hillman parked in one corner of the shopping-centre lot, and drives down the long slope to the beach again, and along past the bay, and north beyond town altogether on a road that twists around rock bluffs and dips through farm valleys and humps through second-growth timber until he turns off suddenly and rattles downhill on a gravel lane to his log cabin where it stands with others near the water's edge.

And now, Strabo Becker poised on his front steps looks back down the strait where the ferry he has just left is nosing its way out again into the open water beyond stony islands and buoys and floating debris. Away, he sings, I'd rather sail a-wa-a-ay. His only song, it is half mumbled this time, or chewed; he's no golden-voiced crooner. He is only a man, he says, and that's more than enough for anyone to be.

And yet this man, this bushy raccoon of a man, with his long narrow red-rimmed eyes calmly filming the world, and his large bent-forward ears silently recording all that the world might say, this man has pretensions. He has chosen to nest on a certain piece of this world and to make a few years of its history his own. The debris of that history is around him and he will reel it all in, he will store it in his head, he will control it; there will be no need, eventually, for anything else to exist; all of it will be inside, all of it will belong only to him. Becker wants to be God.

PRELIMINARY POSE SKETCHES FOR "SEA WATCH"

G 1985

Everlasting

Secret Havens
David Terrell Hellyer

I believe that most of us hold in the mind's eye and memory certain intimate places whether they be a particular room, a secret hiding place behind the hay bales in a barn, a shack or a piece of the outdoors. These places have served as refuges from a world too much with us, as quiet or secret dream spheres where we may pretend everything is as we wish it to be . . . places beyond the critical eye of family or peers. In my life there have been and still are a good many of such precious havens, and almost all of them have been far from the works of man.

My special places have characteristics in common, although they are widely separated geographically and have played important roles over the span of many years. The ground is dry but not parched, carpeted with small plants of many varieties. The grass grows just tall enough to hide a reclining boy or man — for one cannot get close to the earth when sitting in a chair or on a rock or log. Three sides of these small fragrant meadows must be sheltered, whether by boulders, thick brush growing on a bank, but usually by a forest edge. The foreground should slope away gently, but with small shrubs or rocks to define the limits of the immediate domain while not obstructing the wider view.

The more distant prospects may vary greatly so long as they remain in a natural state — a slow running brook, a small alpine lake, a valley, or a range of hills will do. Awe inspiring mountain peaks, the endless curve of the ocean's horizon, the crashing and pounding on waves of rocky shores, the roar of torrent, are not appropriate backdrops to my special places. Sounds must be harmonious and muted like that of a gentle breeze, the hum of nectar-seeking insects, or the chuckling and murmuring of slow-moving water.

One introduces such places only to special friends or a lover — and then anxiously and defensively like an author first exposing a precious work. Silent appreciation and awareness are the appropriate responses. Except for the rare appreciative ones, the best companions on one's visits to such havens are a dog or a horse. Wordlessly the dog will explore the immediate warm, grassy site and, finding it good, look briefly at the farther scene, then turn slowly three times in a counterclockwise circle and bed down with a contented sigh, his back against a rock or bush. The horse, with ears pricked, also looks out to the larger view, then drops his head and starts to clip and munch the forbs and grass, acknowledging the safety and peace of the surroundings.

THE PADDLER

I saw this scene on a beach and the idea for a painting simmered in the back of my mind for about three years. I wanted a home-made kayak and finally found one in Georgian Bay in Ontario. As soon as the model held the paddle comfortably in his hand I realized that my preconceived composition wasn't going to work. Though this composition is unique, I think it is successful. But as so little of the kayak shows, I wonder now why I waited three years to paint it.

Many special places stand out in my mind, although less significantly, like beads on an almost endless string: the tepee site in the Canadian Rockies by the little stream facing Sawbuck Lake with its backdrop of rocks and snowfields, the many camps beneath sycamores and oaks in the coastal range of California, a few dry desert camps, camps in the Cascades and the Olympics, and in the last fourteen years, camps in the Wyoming Wind River Mountains. It was to that special area in Wyoming that I returned.

Forever
W. O. Mitchell

W hen Brian turned he could just pick out the water tower, the gumdrop dome of Lord Roberts School, the spire of the catholic church. All around him the wind was in the grass with a million timeless whisperings.

A forever-and-forever sound it had, forever and for never. Forever and forever the prairie had been, before there was a town, before he had been, or his father, or *his* father, or *his* father before him. Forever for the prairie; never for his father — never again.

People were forever born; people forever died, and never were again. Fathers died and sons were born; the prairie was forever, with its wind whispering through the long, dead grasses, through the long and endless silence. Winter came and spring and fall, then summer and winter again; the sun rose and set again, and everything that was once — was again — forever and forever. But for man the prairie whispered — never — never.

And as the boy stood with the prairie stretching from him, he knew that things were different now — forever and forever — forever the dark well of his mother's loneliness, forever the silence that could never end.

His mother! The thought of her filled him with tenderness and yearning. She needed him now. He could

feel them sliding slowly down his cheek; he could taste the salt of them at the corners of his mouth. There were no catches of breath, simply tears as he stood alone in the silence that stretched from everlasting to everlasting.

A meadowlark splintered the stillness.

The startling notes stayed on in the boy's mind. It sang again.

A sudden breathlessness possessed him; fierce excitement rose in him.

The meadowlark sang again.

He turned and started for home, where his mother was.

FIRST BORN

(overleaf) Without being overly sentimental, I wanted to show the relationship between a mother and her child. To put the emphasis on the child, I used the mother's hand, the baby bag and directional lines. I've done so many painting of weathered cowboys and seamen, I found painting the smooth, line-free skin of a baby a difficult challenge.

THE ARTIST

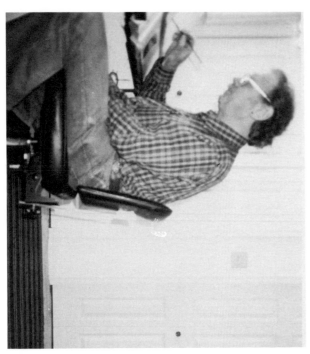

I have known Len Gibbs for twenty years and I have survived! I know what he is really like as a person and as an artist, which in Len's case are always one and the same.

On the historical side I can tell you that he was born in Cranbrook, British Columbia, in 1929, the year of the previous crash. He was raised in the depression, along with his older brother, by a widowed mother in Brandon and later in Edmonton. Today he lives in Victoria, has a wife who is a writer, two grown children, one grandchild, a dog, a cat, several cars and some goldfish . . . in order of importance.

Over the past fifty years he has daily celebrated his existence with the energy and enthusiasm of a Canadian Zorba, and as an afterthought, accomplished every major task that challenged him, except for his art — for that he had to work hard.

Len lives comfortably and at times uneasily with his giant talent, perhaps depending on the moon. He is usually cheerful, sometimes courteous and damned difficult to portray in less than four volumes. If I have the privilege of knowing him for another twenty years I will never see around all his corners . . . but then neither will he.

There are too many Len Gibbs trapped inside that medium-sized body he uses to anchor his floating moustache. Most people who meet Len receive the gift of his humor, usually directed at himself. A very great many have enjoyed his generosity. A few witness his quiet, almost painful sensitivity. To say that he is an accomplished artist and a complex individual is an understatement.

If you watch Len for some time you'll discover he himself is much like his paintings . . . infinite living detail: complex, colorful emotions and vivid dialogue. His smile is really a grin in disguise and his eyes light up and flicker like candles when he talks, memorizing everything he sees.

Now, having said all those nice things, most of which are true, I will tell you that he can be the most exasperating, stubborn and temperamental paint splasher you'll ever meet. Maybe it's the nature of his profession, for when he bursts forth it's like star shells flashing and all those poor ordinary mortals running from the sparks.

He'll deny that but no matter!

When I think back over the years I could probably say that he has always had too much imagination and energy and when he didn't burn it off painting he had to use it up almost outrageously. His life is full of stories which are close to being unbelievable if you don't know him. The force that drives the sea winds drives his red blood, at times like a hurricane.

Len is continuously working, finding components, changing themes. He is never satisfied. He has always been his own heaviest critic, which is at times a burden but always a challenge.

I remember the excitement and some remorse, one late evening, watching Len burn five of his paintings in the fireplace. I recall first the shock, then anger, then the warm heat. "That took courage Len. Pass the wine."

Maybe he was right. Perhaps those paintings were not good enough. If that were to happen today, and for all I know it still does, I can see several gallery owners and collectors hot stepping through the coals to rescue them.

Those days remembered, make the spirit dance again but the greatest excitement is to have witnessed how the appreciation of the art of Len Gibbs has spread.

Len's work deserves to be enjoyed by the largest possible audience. The children whom he sometimes paints enjoy his creations as much as the collectors who snap them up. Enjoy his work, for I am sure you will see something of yourself in the art of Len Gibbs.

Robert G. Evans, Victoria, 1988

In the Artist's Studio

I'm not concerned with fashion, a style of painting is some thing that evolves. Twenty-five years ago I started painting big textured oils with a palette knife but they didn't satisfy what I wanted to say. Most paintings come about as the result of a fleeting impression. I see people doing something that interests me, or the play of light on a surface, perhaps the texture of a tree or a fabric in a certain light, and I do a little doodle in a notebook just as a memory kicker. Later I expand the idea, find the location and the models.

I do a few little sketches to show the model what I want him to be doing, though I don't always have the model in the actual setting that is going to be the background. That's the nice thing about being an artist. I can move elements around or leave out things I don't want. I can move in a tree or a hill, change a red shirt to a blue one, bring in bright light on a cloudy day. Quite often when I'm out with a model, particularly children, they get bored with posing and go off and do their own thing for a while. That sort of happy event often leads to another painting.

With the model I do some fast sketches and take dozens of photographs. A camera is an "instant sketch pad," — a useful tool that saves a lot of time for both the model and the artist.

The sketches, doodles and photographs are pinned up in the studio and I take bits and pieces from them — a good ear from one, a good shoe from another, and work out a composite

This shows the evolution of a painting. In the first sketch, the treeline in the background was subordinate. Eventually the composition changed so that the dark trees dominate.

Some detail sketches of the pose and model.

Finally a water color is done to establish the final composition, light and shadow and color.

The painting is underway, from its first tonal underpainting to the finished work.

drawing. The ability to draw well is the most essential asset that an artist can have.

From there I do several thumb-nail sketches and a preliminary water color. These save me from working myself into nasty traps later on. The final drawing is transferred onto a gessoed panel that has been sanded smooth between coats and then, I do a loose underpainting in watery acrylic. The underpainting records the range of tones from light to dark.

Having worked out the problems of composition, light, shadow and anatomy the real painting begins. I need to have privacy and long periods of uninterrupted time to concentrate on textures and to build life into the work with paint and glazes.

People ask me how long it takes to do a painting and I suppose I could say twenty-five or thirty years because that's how long it took me to learn my craft. Or I could say four or five years, because often an idea simmers on the back burner for a long time. But after I've sketched the idea, found the models, done the thumbnails and preliminaries, drawn the figure, transferred the drawing to a panel, shut the studio door and turned the radio on to light classics, then I'd say anywhere from two weeks to a month.

ACKNOWLEDGEMENTS

Grateful acknowledgement is made for permission to use the following copyrighted material:

Rhythms of the Land, and *Farm Friends* from BUTTER DOWN THE WELL by Robert Collins. Reprinted by permission of Western Producer Prairie Books.

April Passage from THE DOG WHO WOULDN'T BE by Farley Mowat. Used by permission of McClelland and Stewart Ltd.

Spring Breakup and *Silent Ken* from CHILCOTIN HOLIDAY by Paul St. Pierre. Reprinted by permission of Douglas and McIntyre.

Lengthening Shadows and *Forever* from WHO HAS SEEN THE WIND by W. O. Mitchell. Reprinted by permission of Macmillan of Canada, a Division of Canada Publishing Corporation.

Ghostly Dance and *Tell Me about the Winters* from WINTER by Morley Callaghan. Reprinted by kind permission of the author.

Summer Games from RAISINS AND ALMONDS by Fredelle Bruser Maynard, copyright 1964, 1967, 1968 by Fredelle Bruser Maynard. Reprinted by permission of Doubleday and Co. Inc.

School Days from SATURDAY CAME BUT ONCE A WEEK by Peter Shostak. Reprinted by permission of Yalenka Enterprises Inc.

Scars from the book of the same title by W. P. Kinsella reprinted by permission of Oberon Press.

Practical Jokes from WHY SHOOT THE TEACHER by Max Braithwaite. Used by permission of McClelland and Stewart Ltd.

Worn Horseshoes, excerpt from PLEASANT VALLEY by Louis Bromfield, copyright 1943, 1944, 1945 by Louis Bromfield. Reprinted by permission of Harper and Row Publishers Inc.

Two Years Cub from HEADWATERS and *Shawn* from MEN FOR THE MOUNTAINS by Sid Marty, used by permission of McClelland and Stewart Ltd.

Angling excerpt from THE THOUSAND MILE SUMMER by Colin Fletcher, copyright 1964 by Colin Fletcher. Reprinted by permission of Brandt and Brandt, Literary Agents Inc.

The Mustang Colt from THE STUD HORSE MAN by Robert Kroetsch. Reprinted by permission of the author.

Sea Anchor from TROLLER from the short story collection PICKING THE MORNING COLOUR by Kevin Roberts. Reprinted by permission of Oolichan Books.

The Island from ONCE UPON AN ISLAND by David Conover, reprinted by permission of John Hawkins and Associates, literary agents.

Blue Highways from BLUE HIGHWAYS: A JOURNEY INTO AMERICA by William Least Heat Moon, copyright 1982 by William Least Heat Moon. Reprinted by permission of Little, Brown and Co.

Becker from THE INVENTION OF THE WORLD by Jack Hodgins. Reprinted by permission of Macmillan of Canada, a Division of Canada Publishing Corp.

Secret Havens from AT THE FOREST'S EDGE by David Terrell Hellyer. Reprinted by permission of Pacific Search Press.

Something Wonderful from MEN OF THE SADDLE by Andy Russell. Reprinted by permission of Kellock and Associates Ltd., literary agents.

EXHIBITIONS

- 1984, 85, 87 — Royal Institute of Painters in Watercolor, London, England
- 1983, 85, 87 — Canadian Society of Marine Artists, Vancouver and Victoria, British Columbia
- 1984, 86, 87, 88 — Hollander York Gallery, Toronto, Ontario
- 1983 — Alberta Provincial Museum, "Human Heritage"
- 1981 — Prairie Art Gallery, Grande Prairie, Alberta
- 1981 — Beijing, Sichuan, and Shanghai, Travelling Group Show
- 1980 — Province of British Columbia, European Travelling Show
- 1979, 80 — Artist's Choice Show, Roberts Gallery, Toronto, Ontario
- 1976 — 83, 85, 88 — West End Gallery, Edmonton, Alberta
- 1979 — "Preview '79" Dallas, Texas
- 1978 — Peter Whyte Gallery, Banff, Alberta
- 1977 — University of Calgary, "Print and Drawing Council of Canada"
- 1976 — Bradley Gallery, Santa Barbara, California
- 1975 — Mount Allison University, Sackville, New Brunswick, "Acute Images of Canada"
- 1974 — Galerie Royale, Vancouver, British Columbia
- 1973 — Galery Internationale, Ribe, Denmark
- Prior to 1973 he exhibited in Edmonton, Vancouver, Calgary and Ottawa

In 1983, Mr. Gibbs was named Honorary Alberta Artist in recognition of his contribution to the Visual Arts of Alberta and in 1985, was named an Honorary Citizen of Victoria, British Columbia.

COMMISSIONS

Royal Trust Company
Edmonton Symphony
Canadian Northwest Energy Corporation
Beautiful B.C. Magazine
Canada 1
R. Angus Alberta Ltd.
Chieftan Developments Ltd.

COLLECTIONS

Toronto Dominion Bank
Interprovincial Pipelines Ltd.
Edmonton Journal
Canadian Utilities
R. Angus Alberta Ltd.
Lion Business Machines
Waterloo Industries
Jarvis Engineering
Saskatoon Art Gallery
Canadian Western Natural Gas
Pan Canadian Petroleum Ltd.
Gulf Canada
Northwestern Utilities
MacDonald's Tobacco
Bank of Alberta
Highfield Oil and Gas

Bannister Continental
Scott Paper Company
University of Denver
Dofasco Ltd.
Chieftan Developments Ltd.
Shell Resources
Northern Telecom
Syncrude Canada Ltd.
Graceland College, Lamoni, Iowa
Molson Breweries
Medi Centres
Alberta Government Telephones
Grant MacEwan Community College
Allarco Developments
Denton Group

PUBLICATIONS

Yacht Portraits, Overseas Milan, Italy, 1988
The Art of Len Gibbs, Reidmore, 1981
Canadian Art Investors Guide, 1978
Malahat Review, 1978
Western Living, 1977
Southwest Art, U.S.A., 1977
A.M.A. Magazine, 1976
Arts West, 1976
Roundstone Council, "Canadian Artists in Exhibition 1974"
Arts Review, London, England, 1974
Vancouver Playboard, 1974

IMAGES
Type was set in
Times Roman
by
Rebus Composition Systems/
Renown Printing,
Niagara Falls, Ontario.
Printed on
Baskerville Gloss,
and
Byronic Text
by Metropole Litho Inc.,
Anjou, Quebec.
Colour separations
by
Superior Engravers Ltd.